LETTING YOU GO

JORDAN MARIE

Cover Designer by: Sarah Hansen

WARNING: This book contains sexual situations, violence and other adult themes. Recommended for 18 and above.

❀ Created with Vellum

DEDICATION

Letting You Go is a different kind of book for me. It stretched me as a writer and allowed me to explore an avenue I've been wanting to for a while and one you will see so much more of in Book Two. Because of that, I had some special ladies that held my hand and a special shout out is required.

Jenn Allen, Tami Czenkus and Melinda Parker, *you girls have become my MVP's in this game. Thank you for your quick responses, your hand holding and for never failing to keep me on course. Love you ladies.*

Pauline Digaletos *I don't have enough words for you. You give so much and get so little from me. If we lived closer you'd be begging me to leave you alone. I love you.*

Glenna Maynard *my Eastern Kentucky connection, I love you. Thank you for editing, but most of all thank you for taking time out of writing your own kick ass books to be my friend. #LoveYouHard*

Dessure Hutchins *you've had a rough year, but if there is any justice in this world, then, this year will be one of your best because you deserve it.*

Your heart is bigger than Texas, and your spirit shines so bright it cannot dim, even when some idiot tries to stamp it out. Love you!

Finally, to my reading group and all of the girls that are still reading my books after all of these years. I'd be lost without you. Please never stop. I ain't too proud to beg. (You're welcome for the ear worm.)

Xoxo

J

JORDAN'S EARLY ACCESS LINKS

Did you know there are three ways to see all things Jordan Marie, before anyone else?

First and foremost is my reading group. Member will see sneak peeks, early cover reveals, future plans and coming books from beloved series or brand new ones!

If you are on Facebook, it's easy and completely free!

Jordan's Facebook Group

If you live in the U.S. you can **text JORDAN to 797979** and receive a text the day my newest book goes live or if I have a sale.

(Standard Text Messaging Rates may apply)

And finally, you can subscribe to my newsletter!

Click to Subscribe

LETTING YOU GO

Stone Lake Series
Book 1

By:

Jordan Marie

I met Luna Marshall when I was seventeen.

She was a force of nature that I wasn't ready for.

She was gravity and I was caught in her pull—

Powerless, while she held me in a world I was desperate to escape.

They say you never forget your first love.

I believe they're right.

I'll always remember the sound of her laughter.

The way she whispered my name when I touched her, and the taste of her on my lips.

I'll remember everything.

Including the look of pain as I walked away.

CHAPTER ONE

GAVIN

The Beginning

Luna Marshall.

The girl haunts me.

Has for years.

I watch as she stands over by the football bleachers laughing with her friends. Her voice is fucking… musical. It's soft and sweet with a melody in it that somehow brings me peace.

We're complete opposites.

Luna comes from one of the wealthiest families in Stone Lake. Her dad drives a fucking Caddy and her mom has a Lexus SUV. Her clothes are designer and last month she was voted homecoming queen. Krissy Hanes was pissed because she thought the title belonged to her. Normally seniors are always the queen, but Stone Lake allows juniors to run too. Luna is that popular.

Way out of my fucking league.

She is destined to marry the football quarterback or some shit. It's a small town and that's the way these things go.

Except, Luna doesn't date.

She's been asked out a lot. She's been asked out by the football jock, the captain of the debate team, the star basketball player, and the swim team—the entire male swim team. And one by one the alluring Luna Marshall turned them all down.

She's developed the nickname Icebox. The entire male population of our school jokes that if you can ever get your dick inside of her that she'll freeze it off.

They're idiots.

I don't get that from her at all. I think she could burn you alive with her fire and there's a big part of me that craves that heat, wants to tempt fate and take it from her.

She's got long golden blonde hair—the complete opposite of what you would think, given her name. It falls in these soft waves all the way down—the tips resting on the small of her back. Her eyes are green with flecks of brown in them and they sparkle when she laughs. Her lips are full and thick, and I'd be a lying mo-fo if I said I didn't fantasize about having them wrapped around my cock.

I'm seventeen. It's a given that sex is pretty much all I think about and for me... sex is all about Luna Marshall. It's simply my bad luck that it's the same for every damned male in our high school.

Even my own brother.

Atticus is standing near her even now. Sniffing around her, desperate for her attention and she gives it to him—at least more than she has any other male. Maybe that's the one reason I haven't made my move with her. The thing is, when she touches Atticus—like she's doing right now—it's not sexual, it's not any different than she does with her friend Jules. Jules is hot too—also blonde and a rocking body—but, not in the same league as Luna.

Not even close.

Still, she laughs and talks with Atticus but there's no sexual vibe there at all, at least coming from her. I know without a shadow of a doubt he's got his eye on her.

Atticus and I have our own problems, which is fucked. When you have a family like we do, it'd be good to be close, to rely on one another.

We don't.

Our mother hit the road when I was eight and Atticus was seven. My father is a bastard who holds down a day job—although a shitty one—and then comes home and burns his gut with whiskey every night. By the time he's done he barely knows his own name, let alone ours.

I'm a junior in high school. I failed my freshman year and had to repeat it. I'm barely passing now. I hate school, and Stone Lake for that matter. I have plans to get out of this hellhole the minute I graduate. I'm doing it and not looking back. I have nothing holding me here, not even my brother. I wish we were close, but that's not going to happen. He blames me for the way our father is. I blame our mother and that pisses him off even more.

Atticus and I are night and day and I don't see that ever changing. It's Friday and I haven't spoken to him all week. I don't figure that will change either.

Family means nothing. It's not blood that binds you to someone. I don't know much, but I'm smart enough to know it's not blood. My father's blood is running through my veins, for that matter, so is my mother's. That definitely didn't bind them to me in any lasting way.

Not one damn bit.

I'm getting out of here and I'm leaving Stone Lake completely behind.

When I do, I'll have no regrets…

Except maybe that I didn't get a taste of Luna Marshall before I left. Then again, that's probably a good thing.

For both of us.

CHAPTER TWO

LUNA

He's staring at me again. I won't turn around to look, but I can feel the chills that move down my spine. I know he's there.

I always know when Gavin is near.

I'm in love with him. I have been since my first day in high school when I saw him leaning up against the wall talking to his friends. He's tall with broad shoulders, and he has this jet-black hair that he wears a little too long. It falls at the top of his shoulders and is so dark it glistens. He is perfect and that's not really an exaggeration. He has this smile that makes me feel like he's always thinking something deliciously dirty when he looks at me. I don't know what that says about me, but I *like* it.

Gavin's the only boy that's made me feel...Well... *anything.* He excites me, and whenever I'm anywhere near him, I feel completely alive. That's the way it has been for two years.

Of course, in two years I've not spoken one word to him. I've wanted to. I've even come close once or twice, but then I chicken out. Jules thinks I'm insane, and I guess maybe I am. Every day I make up my mind to go and talk to him...

And every day I chicken out.

I'm a mess. I haven't gone on a date with any of the guys who have asked me. I don't want to date anyone but Gavin. He's never going to ask though. I've finally come to that conclusion. He's not interested. He may stare at me, but he hasn't bothered talking to me, not once in two years. If he was the slightest bit interested, surely that would be different. I need to move on and quit mooning over Gavin Lodge.

There are plenty of other fish out there.

Like his brother Atticus. Jules thinks he's even better looking than Gavin. He's not, but he is really cute and funny. He's sweet, and I can tell he likes me. He's asked me out a few times, and I do like him better than the others that have.

I even thought about saying yes. But, how skeezy is that? I can't go out with a guy and wish I was with his brother the whole night. That's just wrong. So, I've kept Atticus firmly placed in the 'friendzone'.

"You should meet up with us tonight, Luna," Atticus says, drawing my attention back to him.

"Meet up?"

"Yeah, at the campground. We're going to camp out and have a big bonfire."

"My mother would freak at the idea of me being outside all night at a co-ed camp out," I laugh.

I'm not joking. If anything, I'm *understating* how my mother would react. I have great parents, the best really. However, I'm their baby girl and there's no way my mom is going to let me camp out all night with boys and no chaperone.

"What if you tell her you're going to stay with me?" Jules asks.

"What do you mean?"

"You can tell your mom that you're staying with me, and I'll tell mine that I'm staying at your house," she says excitedly.

"You think that will work?"

"Of course, it will!" She states that like she thinks I'm being stupid. When obviously it's the other way around.

"And what happens when Mom calls your house to talk to me?"

"We'll make time to call her and tell her we're going to bed early."

"You think that will work?" I ask again like a parrot, because Jules has to be insane. What parent will believe you're going to bed early on a Friday? Especially if you're staying with a friend?

"Totally," she reiterates, physically jumping up and down.

Totally.

"Come on, Luna. I'll take care of you. Honest, it will be okay," Atticus urges me.

I don't want to do this. Even thinking about lying to my parents makes me nervous. Jules is so excited though and all of my friends are staring at me expectantly. If I say no, I'm totally going to be looked at like I'm a chicken. It's hard enough going through high school with the nickname Icebox. The last thing I need is to have them saying I was too scared to go to a camp out.

"Fine..." I mutter, less than convinced.

"Yay!" Jules screams.

"If I get into trouble, I'm going to kill you," I warn her quietly.

She ignores my warning and wraps her arms around me squealing.

I ignore the sinking sensation that this isn't going to end well.

So if my mom catches me and grounds me for the rest of my life... I'll survive...

Right?

Crap.

CHAPTER THREE

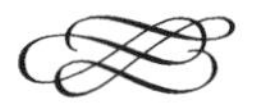

GAVIN

"Where are you going?" I ask Atticus, even though I know I shouldn't. He's been walking around here like his shit doesn't stink all fucking evening.

"A bunch of us are meeting up at the campground for a party," he mutters, throwing some things in an old thin, plastic, store bag.

"Like who?"

"How is it any of your business?"

"I could always tell Dad you're sneaking out." I shrug, being an asshole.

"You're a fucking dick."

"Takes one to know one." I smirk.

"Just a bunch of my friends."

"Like Luna Marshall?" I press.

"Maybe. Why in the hell do you care?"

"She's out of your league. You try to tangle with her and you're asking for trouble," I warn him.

"Is that why you haven't made a move?"

"Don't know what you're talking about," I lie, flopping down on the bed, opening the top of the old zippo lighter I carry around. I strike it, watch the flame, shut it, and then repeat the motion.

"Liar. You've had a hard-on for Luna since day one. You're just too much of a pussy to do anything about it."

"You should be glad I haven't."

"What does that mean?"

"Exactly what I said, little brother. If I made my move on Luna, you wouldn't stand a chance."

"In your dreams. Luna Marshall doesn't want anything to do with you."

"Maybe I'll show up at your party and prove you're a liar."

"You show up tonight, Luna won't have a thing to do with you," he says. He doesn't look at me, instead he stuffs the rest of his junk in the bag and heads to the window.

He might not be looking at me, but I'm keeping my eyes on him, and I can see the fear and nervousness that moves over his face. He's worried. He'd rather kill me than have me show up at the campground tonight.

I really shouldn't. It's stupid. I actually agree with Atticus. Luna Marshall is way out of my league too. I don't want her hooking up with my brother though. Luna might not be meant for me, and I've come to terms with that. I can live with it.

I don't think I could live with the fact she hooked up with my brother.

I don't care if that does make me a dick.

As the window slams and Atticus disappears down the willow tree, there's a voice in my head warning me not to do something stupid.

I ignore it.

CHAPTER FOUR

LUNA

It was a mistake.

A big one.

I look around at all of my friends sitting around the fire, laughing and drinking, having fun, while I mainly want to leave. Jules is wasted and sitting in some guy's lap. I've seen him before, but I don't really know him, and I don't think Jules does either. If I had my own vehicle, I'd hit the road now. Heck, if I had my license, I'd take Jules' car. That's how desperate I am. I'm not having fun, and I keep looking at the road, scared my parents will show up at any moment.

Okay, I realize I'm a goody-two shoes. I do, but, that's just who I am. I like pleasing my parents. They're good to me. I like cheerleading and making good grades. I enjoy being hopelessly boring. The only time I've ever wanted to take a chance and color outside the lines, to be wild... was when I saw Gavin.

Gavin makes me feel reckless. He makes me want to be something else—*someone* else. He makes me want to throw caution to the wind and enjoy every minute of it. Gavin might be worth it. I'd risk having my parents show up in the middle of the night, mad, yelling at me, and grounding me for the rest of my life for Gavin.

Not for this.

"Here ya' go, Luna," Atticus says, coming to sit beside me and handing me a beer.

I don't drink. Jules and I had some wine coolers a couple of times when her parents were out of town. It was fruity and I liked them. They were also purple, which is my favorite color. Beer tastes gross. I'm pretty sure my dog could pee in a beer and it wouldn't change the taste at all. Still, I take it with a fake half-smile.

"Thanks, Attie."

"It's a good night, right?"

"Yeah."

"It doesn't sound like you're having fun," he says.

"I am. Just a little worried about my parents, I guess."

"Parents are a drag."

"Mine aren't. Not really. They're cool, which is probably why I don't like lying to them."

"Relax. It's not like they'll find out. You and Jules already called them, right? And she called hers?"

"Well, yeah. But I keep worrying. Like, what if one of my parents or Jules's is in an accident? What if the house catches on fire? So, they try to find us and discover we lied. My father could have a heart attack or something. My mom would be a worried mess, and then she'd know I wasn't where I said I was, and she'd panic while already being upset..."

"You're a freak, Luna. Breathe. None of that's going to happen," he reassures.

"Yeah, probably not," I tell him. "But that doesn't make me forget the possibility is there."

"At least your parents care about you. My father won't even notice I'm gone and wouldn't for days, if then."

"Of course, he would."

"No. I don't have your kind of life, Luna. Dad barely talks to me. He's drinking from the time I get home from school until he passes out. I don't know how he manages to keep his job at the garage. Old Mr. Gilroy threatens to fire him at least once a week. He just never follows through."

"I'm so sorry, Attie. I had no idea," I whisper, putting my hand on his leg in silent support.

"It's okay. I'm used to doing things on my own. I don't need anyone."

"Well, you have your brother, Gavin. It's good you both have each other."

"Yeah, good ole' Gavin. He's—"

"Late to the party."

My head jerks up at that deep voice and my body experiences an all over shiver. Gavin is standing across from me and Atticus. It's dark, but the light from the fire highlights him perfectly. He's wearing jeans and a flannel shirt that I've seen him in often. It has different colors of blues and greens in it, and I love it because it somehow makes his dark hair appear like it shines.

"What are *you* doing here?" Atticus says, and his voice is laced with anger. I've never seen Atticus upset at anything or anyone. He's always been laid back and easy going. The change in his demeanor is shocking.

"You invited me. Remember?" Gavin says, and something about his smile tells me that is not the full story.

"I remember telling you that there was no way you'd get what you wanted. You might as well go back home now."

"I don't think so. I'm just now starting to enjoy the view," he says and this time when he smiles, he looks right at me.

My heart beats frantically in my chest. It's a dangerous smile. I kind of feel like I'm Little Red Riding Hood and Gavin is the Big Bad Wolf.

"Hey, Luna," he says.

Oh my God! Oh my God! My brain screams as my palms go

sweaty. If I thought my heart was beating hard before, it's thumping like a runaway train now.

Oh. My. God.

Gavin Lodge spoke to me!!?!!

And he knows my name. *Mine.*

Holy freaking cow!

"Uh... Hi.... Gav... Gavin."

Heat explodes through me and centers on my face as I blush so deeply that I probably glow from it.

Can I be any lamer?

I barely could get his name out and my voice cracked. I want to die in shame. I want the ground to swallow me up and bury me alive.

"Want to go for a walk?" he asks, and I blink.

"Me?" I squeak.

"Don't see anyone else here I'd be asking, Babe. Unless you and my brother are busy?"

Oh my God. Gavin is asking me to walk with him. He wants to be alone with me!

Every freaking dream I've ever had has centered on this guy and he just asked to be alone with me.

Me!

"Attie? Um... No. We don't have anything going on. I mean... We're merely friends. We were talking that's all. You know..."

I have got to get control of my nerves. I'm not making any sense, Gavin probably thinks I'm insane. He's probably already regretting asking me to go on a walk.

I expect him to tell me he changed his mind, but then he reaches his hand out.

"Then, take a walk with me, Babe."

I put my hand in his and watch wide-eyed as his fingers wrap around mine and he pulls me up.

His hand is warm, strong and I memorize the feel of it.

I'll remember how it molded to mine for the rest of my life.

CHAPTER FIVE

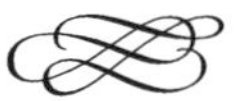

GAVIN

I shouldn't have done this...

That's the one thing I keep thinking as Luna and I walk away from Atticus. It doesn't even help to see the annoyance and anger that flashes over his face.

This is a mistake.

A huge one.

I know that by how great it feels to hold Luna's hand and the rightness I experience in my chest at finally having her close. It might be a mistake that I never recover from.

I have plans after I graduate. They're plans that don't include a woman, they can't. I don't have anything to offer one.

Not yet.

One day, I will. One day I'll work my ass off to have the kind of life I've always wanted. When I get to that point, I'll be ready to have a woman in my life like Luna. One that's sweet and pretty. One that smells good and blushes when she laughs. One that makes a man want dreams and plans.

I'm definitely not that kind of man right now. Which means I should run fast and hard away from her. Luna's not like the other girls. She has forever stamped all over her.

"It's a nice night," she says after we've walked for a bit. I don't know why I do it, but I lead her down to the old wooden boat dock at the edge of the lake. The wood has seen better days, but it's still sturdy. I let go of her hand, ignoring the urge to take it back in mine, and sit down. She does the same, sitting close, but we still have a couple of feet between us. I don't like it, and I immediately want her closer, but the distance is good.

I stare out over the water, not replying to her—unsure of what to say.

It's definitely a mistake being here alone with her.

"I didn't know you knew my name," she says, trying again. She's not looking at me, she's gazing out at the water. I can't see her face clearly, despite the full moon above us. If I had to guess though, I'd say she was blushing because I can hear the embarrassment in her voice. It makes me feel like an asshole.

"I shouldn't have done this."

"Done what?" she asks.

"Came out here with you. We don't fit, Luna."

"What?"

"I've known your name since the day you walked down the hall and smiled at me, Luna. You were a freshman and so damn pretty you got my attention right away. I've watched you every day of every year since then. You have to know that."

"I do," she says, her voice dropping down into a near whisper. "But you never spoke to me. I thought maybe..."

"Maybe what?" I ask her when she doesn't finish.

"I thought maybe I was imagining it because I wanted it so much. I wanted you to like me."

"You shouldn't."

"What?" she asks, confused.

I turn to her and she's looking at me. In the moonlight, I can see the way her forehead crinkles with uncertainty, and I think it's cute, even if I shouldn't. Then again, I think everything about Luna Marshall is cute.

"We don't fit," I repeat.

"You said that before, but I don't understand."

"You're uptown, Luna. You live in a big house on a hill with a picket fence and a three-car garage."

"So?"

"So, I live in a house that could probably fit in your garage. My dad walks to work because he had his license revoked for driving drunk. He comes home and drinks the night away. You eat dinner with your parents every night. Atticus and I fix a peanut butter or a bologna sandwich because that's what we buy from the jobs we go to after school."

"That doesn't matter to me."

"It wouldn't because you have no idea what it's like to live the life I do. But I know the real world, Luna, and your kind and mine don't match."

"I think we match," she says shyly, ignoring my warnings. She even manages to get brave and slides her hand back in mine. I want to pull away. Instead, I thread my fingers through hers.

"Your parents won't. If you ever try to bring me to that fancy house on the hill, you'll see."

"I guess we'll just have to see what happens, won't we?" she asks.

Unease rises up inside of me when she smiles. Her face is full of happiness that shines bright, despite the darkness. I don't understand what just happened. She should be running the other way. Instead....

It feels like she just claimed me.

CHAPTER SIX

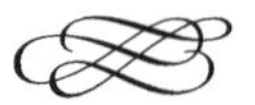

LUNA

"Gavin?" I whisper.

The moon has completely disappeared behind the clouds and the sound of the water sloshing gently against the dock, combined with the crickets chirping and the darkness brings an eerie feeling. My heart rate kicks into overdrive, and I wonder if I can make it back to the party despite the black. I'm not even sure what direction to start. "Gavin!" I call out again, this time slightly louder—but not too loud. I'm an avid watcher of horror films, and it's always the girl who acts like an idiot, screaming and panicked, that gets slaughtered.

I'd rather not have slaughtered written in my obituary.

"Relax Luna. I'm here," Gavin says. His voice has the magic ability to make me instantly relax.

"I got scared when you weren't here," I mumble, feeling only slightly embarrassed. Then I see him walking through a large clump of trees, carrying a small flashlight, and he's holding... *my blanket.*

I smile.

"I went back to get a blanket. I didn't want you to get cold."

"That's sweet," I tell him, suddenly feeling warm all the way to my toes.

"Not really, I was cold too," he says, stopping as he gets next to me. He's got a different look to him than normal. At school he's always looked so cocky—like he doesn't have a care in the world. He always gives off the bad boy who will break your heart vibe, full force. Here, like this, he looks relaxed, self-assured but not arrogant, just... *real.* After years of viewing him as someone akin to a rock star, it's a huge difference.

He's... *normal*—incredibly good looking, cute, sexy and funny, but normal.

He could definitely be on the pages of Seventeen magazine and look better than anyone they've ever used. But still, he's ... normal... *real.*

And I think he likes me.

Me!

He sits down on the dock beside of me. I watch as he bunches up his jacket and puts it on the dock. Then, he spreads the blanket over both of our legs. Finally, he turns the flashlight off, throwing us back into the dark. Somehow, it doesn't seem as scary with Gavin beside me.

My eyes adjust and I watch as he shuffles around, finally settling by lying down, his head on his jacket. His arm goes around my waist and he pulls me, so I lay too, positioning us so that I'm facing the lake, my back to his front. He holds me tightly pressed against his body.

I've never lain like this before. Spooned, warm and safe, tightly held, so close that I can feel his breath fall against my hair, as his arm cushions my head. I close my eyes and drink it in. Committing the entire moment to memory. I don't ever want to forget it.

Ever.

"What was everyone doing back at the campsite?" I ask, not really caring, but wanting to hear Gavin's voice some more.

"Still partying. Although your friend Jules was asleep and drooling on Randy."

"I don't know Randy," I mumble, figuring that was the guy she was with earlier.

"He's an asshole."

"Maybe I should—"

"Your girl is safe enough. She's not alone with him, besides he's an asshole, but he won't hurt her."

I frown, still not sure, but Gavin seems like he is, and I don't want to move from the warmth of his body, so I let it go.

"I didn't know you had a flashlight. That was smart."

"I keep one on my keyring. So, not that smart. It would have been smart if I'd brought a sleeping bag or a pillow," he jokes.

"Probably," I grin. "Still it's nice. I love this lake."

"Me too. I come out here and sit on this dock to get away from Atticus and Dad. It's peaceful."

"You and Atticus don't get along?"

"Not in the slightest."

"How come?"

"That's the hundred-dollar question, Babe. But I don't want to waste time talking about my dick-head brother tonight. Not when I'm here with you," he says, kissing the top of my head. I smile so hard that it could almost be painful.

"Fair enough," I murmur, wondering if you can die from so much happiness.

"Are you sweet on my brother?"

"What?"

"You got a thing for him?"

"Of course not. If I did, I wouldn't be out here with you," I assure him.

"Some girls like to play games."

"I don't."

"I didn't think so," he answers.

"Then why did you ask?"

"Because, I wanted to make it clear. Although, if I'm honest, he might be better for you than I am."

"Why do you say that?"

"He's more of what you want, Luna."

"I think I know more of what I want than you do, Gavin."

"I know you," he says and for some reason the way he says it, makes it feel like maybe he does. I turn over on my back so I can see him.

"You're so sure?"

"You're a forever kind of girl. You don't look at the present and just let things be enough, Luna. You plan, you dream."

"You make it sound like there's something wrong with dreaming," I state, not bothering to tell him he's wrong. He's not. I do plan. I do dream. I've been dreaming about him for years.

"Nothing wrong with dreams, Luna. I have a few of my own," he says, leaning up on his elbow to look down at me. His hand moves along the side of my face and I swear I can feel his fingers heat my skin.

"Then, what's wrong with the fact that I plan and dream?"

"Why do you have the nickname Icebox?" he asks, instead of answering.

I frown, my body stiffening at his question.

"I don't like that name," I warn him.

"I guess that means you know why you got it?"

"Larry Richards started spreading it around after I wouldn't go to prom with him," I mumble, anger and humiliation mixed in with my explanation. I hate the nickname. I let on like it doesn't bother me, but it does. The fact that Gavin knows about it makes it worse. No girl wants the boy she likes to know that kind of stuff about her.

"Why didn't you go to the prom with him?" he asks.

"I didn't want to."

"But you went to the prom on your own. No date, right? I thought you girls loved having prom dates."

"I would have liked going to prom with a guy I liked. I don't like Larry."

"He's the football star quarterback."

"He's also a douche canoe," I argue.

Gavin laughs. "You'll get no argument from me."

"Then you should know why I didn't go out with him."

"Fair enough, but the point is you could have gone out a million times the last two years and you shot every last one down."

"That doesn't mean I'm cold," I mutter.

Words are powerful. They wound you deeply. People thought they were being funny and cute. But, every time I heard someone call me that, it felt like I was swallowing down rusty metal—and choking on it.

"I didn't think it did," he says, but that's when something occurs to me. Something so horrible it feels painful only thinking it.

"Is that what this is about?" I ask, pulling away to look at him.

"This?"

"Did you just invite me out here to see if you could *'defrost the icebox'*, Gavin?"

"Guess you've heard that talk, too," he responds, but at least he doesn't sound like he's laughing at me. He even sounds a little... pissed.

"Half the boys that ask me out do so on a dare and a bet."

"I'm not one of those boys, Luna. Don't get me twisted up with them in that pretty head of yours."

"Okay," I answer quietly, noting that he doesn't sound a little pissed now. Gavin is simply angry.

"Larry Richards needs his ass kicked," he mutters, and I don't respond to that—mostly because I feel that way too.

"You're upset," I dare to mention.

"Well, yeah, I am. I just meant to show you that you were

waiting for Mr. Perfect to come along and he doesn't exist. Your dreams and mine are way too different."

"I wasn't waiting for Mr. Perfect, Gavin."

"Who were you waiting on then?" he asks.

I want to tell him the truth. I want to confess that I've been waiting for him, but I don't. He probably would think I'm insane then—or run the other way.

"Mr. Perfect-For-Me."

He looks at me stunned for a minute before his lips spread into a full grin. I can see them perfectly from the light of the moon that's come back out from behind the clouds. I see him and he's beautiful. I've never seen anything more beautiful than Gavin smiling at me like this and his eyes crinkling in the corners.

"What are your dreams, Gavin?" I ask him.

"Not waiting around for Mr. Perfect-For-Me, I can tell you that."

"That's good, because he's going to be a little busy with me if he ever shows up."

"I..." he stops when he realizes what I said and it seems impossible, but that grin deepens.

"It takes a lot of work to defrost an icebox, you know."

"Smart ass." he laughs, leaning down, and my eyes seem to get trapped in his heated gaze. His head bends down closer and my breath stalls in my chest.

This is it.

This is the moment I've been waiting for my entire life.

Gavin Lodge is going to kiss me.

My very first kiss.

My eyes start to close, as I tilt up towards him.

And then....

Gavin kisses my forehead.

Disappointment feels like a living thing inside of me. I swallow it down and the hurt I feel too. I'm left feeling confused, and I pull back to ask Gavin what's going on, but he wraps a strand of my hair around his finger, not allowing me to withdraw.

"You're dangerous, Luna," he whispers. I frown in response, having no idea what he means.

Before I can ask, he shifts us so that I'm once again lying on my side and he's spooning me as we look out over the lake. We lie in silence like that for a bit, and I enjoy being in his arms. That's enough for now.

It has to be.

"The moon is beautiful," I whisper sometime later and more to myself than Gavin. He's been quiet for so long now, that I figure he might be asleep.

"Whenever I look at the moon," he responds, "I always think of you."

"Because of my name." I smile, liking his answer.

"Everyone looks up at the sky and wishes on the stars, gets lost in them, but it's the moon that is the queen. The moon controls so much, keeps everything in balance and she does it without realizing it, without drawing attention to herself."

"That makes you think of me?"

"Trust me, Luna. The moon may have a gravitational pull that controls the ocean, but your pull is just as strong."

His words move through me slowly, sinking in. They feel huge. They feel deep and thoughtful and they're so beautiful I can't wrap my mind around them. We fall silent for a little longer. I can feel myself drifting off to sleep, but before I do, I have to ask one more time.

"What are your dreams, Gavin?"

"To graduate and leave Stone Lake and the entire state of Maine behind in my dust."

"Where would you go?" I ask, hating the idea of him leaving.

"Anywhere the road takes me," he says.

"You wouldn't miss Stone Lake?"

"Not even a little. Although after tonight…"

"Yeah?" I whisper.

"After tonight, I'll miss the lake part of it for sure," he says.

I look out over the water and think about his answer, but Gavin's not done.

"And I'll miss a beautiful girl with sunny blonde hair and green eyes, who feels really good in my arms."

"Gavin..."

"And I know that whenever I look up at the moon, I'll never fail to think of her."

I like that. I like that he says it, and more importantly, that he feels that way.

I like it a lot... but at the same time, for some reason, it makes me unbearably sad.

I don't know how to respond. So, I say nothing.

Eventually, I fall asleep and I do it in Gavin's arms. He might want to leave Stone Lake behind, but as for me, right now I want nothing more than to stay here forever.

Here, in Gavin's arms.

CHAPTER SEVEN

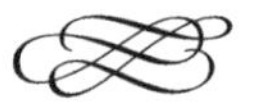

LUNA

"I can't believe you spent the night with Gavin Lodge!" Jules squeals.

I blush, feeling warm all the way through. I look down at my hands and I smile. I can't stop myself from grinning. Gavin held my hand. I laid my head on his shoulder. He talked to me. He likes me. But...

"What if he goes back to ignoring me, Jules?" I ask, terrified that he will. Terrified that Friday night was merely a fluke.

He didn't kiss me. He had to know he could. He didn't even try. We stayed out alone all night, hugged up together on the dock and he didn't try... *anything.* That can't be normal. It wouldn't be with any other guy I know and not only because I've become a challenge to see who can *"defrost"* me. Besides Gavin was held back a year. He's a year older than me and the guys in my classes. I know it's a year, but he has to be used to girls who...

Aren't scared virgins like I am.

An insecure virgin.

"Oh, come on! No guy like Gavin Lodge is going to spend the night with you and not follow up. Not happening chick, especially if he didn't hit it."

"I—"

"Oh my God! You didn't give him your V-card did you, Luna?"

"No," I mutter.

"You so should have. I would if I were you. Gavin has to be better than Toby Drysen who I gave mine too," she says with a sigh.

"He didn't even try to get to second base, let alone punch my V-card," I confess, almost lying. What I tell her is the truth, but it's not quite. I'm kind of sketchy on exactly what first, second and third base are. I'm pretty sure that Gavin didn't even try to get to first base though. I don't want to tell Jules that, so I tell her he didn't try to hit second. I have no idea about any of this crap, but I don't want to look stupid. I get whispered about enough. People think I'm a freak. *I'm not.* I just want my first time to be with someone I love.

With Gavin.

I'm not a cold fish, and I'm definitely not clinging to my virginity.

"He didn't even try to touch you?" she asks, sounding way too surprised. She stares at me, and I feel so uncomfortable I squirm on my bed.

Obviously, we made it back from the campout without my parents finding out and the end of the world happening. It's Saturday night now and Jules is sleeping over at my house and we've vegged out watching movies and scarfing down popcorn and candy all evening. I wish it was Sunday. I already want to see Gavin again, and I know that's not going to happen until time for school. I'm scared about what's going to happen, but I can't wait either. I'm a spaz.

The thought makes me smile and I look down at my hand.

The hand that Gavin held...

I keep repeating that, mostly because I can't get over it. My hand feels different. Sometimes I can almost feel Gavin's hold... even now.

"Luna?"

"What?" I ask, totally distracted and imagining Gavin's hand on mine.

"Did he try to touch you?"

"Of course. I mean he held my hand and he kept his hand on my stomach the whole night, holding me close to him," I tell her, my voice sounding more than a little dreamy as I think of the way he held me.

"He didn't feel you up?"

"What?"

"He didn't like grab your boob? Put his hand down your pants? *Nothing*?" she asks, clearly not impressed.

Those insecurities I've been having all come raging to life full force now.

"Well... no."

"That's not good," she mutters.

"It's not?" I ask, panic thick inside of me as my heart squeezes painfully in my chest.

"Not at all? A guy like Gavin who is rumored to have been with over half the girls at Garrad County High? So not good, Luna."

I ignore her words about the many girls that Gavin has probably slept with and how bad that makes me feel. Instead, I let the fact that she's obviously thinking something is wrong as well to feed my panic.

"Do you think it means he's not really interested in me?" I confess my biggest fear.

"I don't know," she says, almost guiltily.

"Crap," I moan, and I fall headfirst on the bed, burying my face in my pillow, suddenly wanting to cry.

"I mean you would think he'd have to be interested to single you out," she soothes, trying to reassure me. I feel my hope trying to come back to life and then, the next instant, Jules snuffs it out. "Unless he was just trying to piss off Atticus."

"Attie? How would asking me to go off with him piss Attie off?" I ask, thoroughly confused.

"Girl, please. Don't tell me you haven't noticed the way Atticus moons over you."

"He does not," I deny, but I do it while blushing, because I know Atticus has a crush on me. But, he's only a friend and after last night with Gavin, that's all he could ever be.

"Get real. You know better," she laughs, not buying my denial in the slightest.

"We're just friends," I mumble.

"Maybe on your end. But Atticus and Gavin hate each other. The whole school knows that."

"Yeah, I think they might."

"So, there's only one solution," Jules announces.

"What's that?" I ask, desperately wanting to do whatever I can so that Gavin doesn't slip through my fingers.

He's the one for me. *I love him.* I can be the girl who gives him the happiness that he doesn't get because of his dad now. I can fix everything wrong in his life and show him how great our lives will be together. Then, he'll want forever plans, too.

I just know it.

"You have to flirt with Atticus."

"I will.... Wait. *What?*"

"You have to make Gavin jealous so he will notice you and claim you as his. You have to let him think you might go to Atticus if he doesn't pay you attention," she plots, nodding her head for emphasis.

"I can't do that, Jules," I respond, shaking my head.

"You gotta. It's the only way to handle boys. You have to make them want what belongs to someone else."

She sounds so positive.

I get this sick feeling in my stomach.

I want Gavin. I want him so much... but...

"What if I do it with someone else besides Atticus? What about Larry?"

"No. It has to be Atticus. There's competition there. Remember how Atticus always talks about Gavin being held back a year and forced to be in the same grade with him? They compete over everything. Nope. If you want Gavin, you're going to have to flirt with his brother."

I fall back into my pillow, completely deflated and full of despair.

Crap.

CHAPTER EIGHT

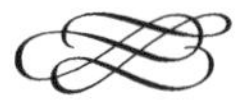

GAVIN

"I guess you're proud of yourself," Atticus growls as I walk into the bedroom.

I ignore him and flop down on the hard, twin mattress of my bed, grab a baseball that is sitting on the nightstand and start tossing it up in the air, catching it.

Our beds used to be bunks, but we separated them years ago—his moved on one side of the room and mine all the way against the wall on the other side. They're as far apart as we can physically get them, and if there was another bedroom, or hell, even room in the garage, they would be even farther apart. I think it kind of symbolizes how our relationship is.

"You just couldn't stay away from Luna, could you? Had to make your play because you knew that I liked her."

He's not wrong. I couldn't stay away from her, and I hated that my brother was getting close to her. I could watch her with anyone but him—at least that's what I tell myself. The truth is, seeing Luna with any guy would probably piss me off.

"Talk to me, damn you!" he yells.

The only thing that Atticus and I have ever agreed on, is the mutual hate of our father. It's a dick move, but since he wants me to talk, I decide to point out the obvious.

"You sound just like our father right now."

"You bastard," he snarls then launches himself at me. I'd just caught the baseball and I hurl it toward him in reflex. It hits him on the shoulder, bouncing off to crash against the window. The sound of glass shattering registers for nearly a second before Atticus's body connects with mine and his fist slams under my chin. The force of the blow jerks my head up, and I ignore the pain as I connect with Atticus's ribs. We trade blows, and I throw him off of me. He crashes on the floor but gets right back up and charges again. I fall back, hitting the table by my bed. It scrapes against the worn, hardwood floors. I feel the edge of the wood cut into my back, as I push back against Atticus.

We're pretty evenly matched. I'm a little taller than him and maybe a little broader but blow for blow we're not that different. I might be the first to draw blood, but his next punch cuts my lip and the coppery, bitter taste of it hits my tongue.

"What the fuck?"

Atticus and I both freeze solid as our father storms into the room. His question is surprisingly sober, no slurring at all. When I look up however, I can tell he's been drinking. His salt and pepper hair is mussed and sticking up in a million different directions. He hasn't shaved in a few days and the scruff is mostly gray. He's wearing a torn white t-shirt that has oil stains on it and barely covers his growing beer belly. There's a bottle in his hand too. Our father might be wondering what was going on in his sons' room, but not enough to put down his drink.

"You two assholes cut down the racket. A man can't even enjoy his drink around here anymore. Keep this shit up and you'll find yourselves on the street. It'd serve you right. You're getting too old to depend on me for a roof over your head. That's not the way the world works."

I hate him.

I. *Hate*. Him. That's all there is to it. He hasn't paid one bill on this place in so long that I can't remember the last time he did. The only groceries he buys would be alcohol and maybe the stray loaf of bread. That's it, but yet he acts like we owe him everything. I don't know what the future holds, but I know that whatever it is, I want it to be far away from him.

I wasn't lying when I told Luna my kind and hers don't mix. This is just more proof.

He turns away from us and walks out of the room, staggering.

That's dear old dad in a nutshell.

I loosen my hold on Atticus's shirt and shove him away from me. He goes, not bothering to keep fighting, and I'm glad.

"You should have left her alone," he mutters as we're picking up the shit that fell to the floor while we were fighting. I'll have to find some cardboard to put over the window. Tomorrow I'll find a piece of wood. There's no way in hell my father will repair it—that much I know.

"I know, but I couldn't," I respond, knowing I shouldn't.

"Because of me," he accuses.

I let out a deep breath wishing like fuck I could leave Stone Lake behind tonight.

After graduation.

I have to keep reminding myself of that. Soon, I can leave everything behind. The odd thing is now when I think of doing that, Luna's face flashes in my mind.

"Because I couldn't stop myself," I tell Atticus, flopping back on my bed after retrieving my baseball. I should shut up, but instead here I am talking to my asshole brother and sharing more than I should.

"You won't keep her, even if you have her right now. She's too good for you, Gav. There's no way you can keep her," he says, and I can hear the pleasure in his voice. The dumbass thinks he's getting to me by telling me that shit. I throw my ball up in the air, ignoring him. I already know I can't keep Luna. I already know she's not mine to keep.

No matter how much I might want to.

CHAPTER NINE

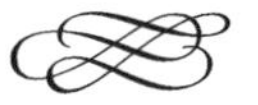

LUNA

Walking through the halls of school, it feels like everyone is staring at me. I don't know why they would, but it still feels that way. I tried to smile at a few people, but they would jerk their heads away and look in the opposite direction, almost as if they were ashamed to be caught gawking at me.

It's making me self-conscious. I don't know what's going on. Part of me is hoping it's mostly in my head. I make it to my locker and breathe a sigh of relief when I can hide behind the metal door. I sift through my books to find the one that I need for my next class. I'm so nervous that I fumble the book in my hand, and it falls to the floor. I close my eyes and take a breath, needing to get control and calm myself.

I know what's wrong—well, besides the fact everyone is acting strange. It's that the day is half over, and I've not seen Gavin once.

Not once.

I thought maybe he was absent, but Jules has study hall with him in first period and she said he was there. I waited like a fool in front of my locker this morning, hoping against hope he would show up looking for me. He didn't and I shrugged it off, figuring he had no real idea where my locker was. As the day moved on and I never saw him—not even in passing, not even standing by the water fountains where he usually was—this uneasiness just kept growing in my stomach.

I feel... stupid.

Obviously, Friday night, which meant so much to me, didn't mean anything to him. Maybe he was only lonely. Maybe it did have to do with his brother. Jules apparently thinks it does. She keeps urging me to flirt with Atticus to keep Gavin's interest. I'd be lying if I said I wasn't tempted, but I don't want to do that. Atticus has been really nice to me, but I don't like him—not like he wants me to. I wouldn't want to use him either. That's just not right.

"Hey, Luna."

I jerk up when I hear Larry's voice.

Here I was thinking today couldn't get any worse.

I finish putting things into my locker and getting what I need out before closing the door.

"Larry," I respond, turning to look at him.

"How are you doing, Luna?"

"I'm good," I grumble, barely resisting the urge to add that I was better before he got here.

"You got a date for the Mayday Dance?"

Shit.

"Nope, I wasn't planning on going."

"You're the captain of the cheerleading squad," he says, and I frown because I have no idea what that has to do with anything.

"Larry, I need to get to class—"

"It won't look right if you don't go to the Mayday Dance."

"To who?"

"To everyone, Luna," he responds, and I wonder if he realizes how whiney his voice can sound. "How about we go together?"

"I don't think that would be a good idea," I tell him. "I really better get to class. I'll talk to you later—"

"Come on, Luna. Don't be like that," he says, grabbing my arm and pulling me back around to face him. His hold is hard, with a bruising force, shocking me.

"Let go of me," I gasp.

"Come on, the whole school is talking about how easily you gave it up for Gavin Lodge."

I jerk my arm, trying to get free. I'm so intent on getting away from him that at first, I miss what he said...*and then it hits me.*

"Let me... What did you say?"

"If I'd known you like to go slumming, I would have handled you differently, Luna."

"Go... Handled me..." I'm sputtering, not really knowing what to say. My stomach twists and turns and I can feel bile rising. I knew it.

I knew it.

I knew it felt like the entire school was looking at me differently.

"Lodge has been bragging about it to everyone. He said you caught on fire for him. If you like it dirty, Luna, I can give it to you even better than him. There's no reason for you to look on the poor side of town."

I shove against him now, his words disgusting me.

"Get away from me!"

His hold tightens for a brief moment before his fingers rake against my skin, making it burn as he draws blood. I cry out from the pain, looking up at him, and that's when I see Gavin launching his body into Larry, taking him down on the floor.

I step away from them a few feet, holding my wounded arm and staring in awe as Gavin starts hitting Larry repeatedly.

CHAPTER TEN

GAVIN

"You fucking bastard," I growl, slamming my fist over and over into Larry. I don't let up either; I whale on him. When I saw him grab Luna and heard the pain in her voice, I saw red.

I fucking lost it.

I charged at him, forgetting everything else. All I want now is to hurt him for the way he just hurt Luna. That's all I have on my mind as I hit Larry repeatedly. Punching him so hard that the skin on my knuckles is cut. I feel someone pulling on my body, trying to drag me off of him. I fight them too. I don't let go of my target. I've had a lot of frustration and misery over the years and right now I decide to unload it all.

Directly on his face. Fucking asshole.

Eventually, they pull me from him, my energy too driven, too spent to fight more than one foe at a time. I begin to let my surroundings filter back in. That's when I hear Luna crying, and see the crowd gathering around us. Principal Issacs is talking, but I don't make his words out. They're drowned out by the amplified sound of the blood rushing and pounding in my ears and Luna's tears. I try to go to her, to stop them, but the principal grabs me by the arm. I could probably take him—I'm pretty sure about it, but he has the security officer with him.

"Luna," I demand, wanting to talk to her.

She lifts her head to look at me. Her skin is pale, tears are running unchecked down her cheeks, and a look of betrayal on her face that I don't think I'll ever erase from my mind.

"Gavin," she says, her voice thick with tears.

"Alright, boys, let's get to the office," the principal says.

"Luna—"

"Why Gavin?" she asks, and I frown, confused.

I can't tell her why Larry hurt her. I figure it's mostly because he's an asshole and she probably already knows that.

I want to stay with her, to talk to her, but they're pulling me away.

"I'll be back," I tell her, needing to reassure her. "I'll find you when I get done," I add when she doesn't reply.

I watch as my brother comes up and puts his arm around her shoulder—giving her comfort when it should be me. I try to jerk away from the principal again.

Bastard.

I feel jealousy slide through me with the force of a runaway train. I pull against the principal's hold, needing to get him away from her.

"Get your damn hands off of her," I growl.

"Don't you think you've done enough, Gavin?" Atticus sneers.

I'm so fucking confused. I know it shows on my face, but I can't figure out what's going on here. Luna is looking at me with so much pain that I don't understand anything.

"Luna—"

"Luna doesn't want anything to do with you anymore. I hate that you're my brother. I know you thought it was a game to get Luna to stay the night with you. You thought you would hurt me by using her, but this is low even for you, Gavin. Did you have fun spreading it all over the school that you slept with her? Did you get off on destroying her reputation? You're lucky the principal is here to save you, or I'd kill you!"

"What in the fuck—" I bark the words, breaking off to lunge at my worthless brother for even thinking I'd do that. I hear Luna cry out as I'm pulled back again—by both the security guard and the principal. Their holds are like vices, and I have no hope of resisting. Still, I don't turn around, I keep fighting them. "Let me go! Luna, I didn't do that. You have to believe me," I yell.

She looks at me, but all I can see are her tears. Atticus pulls her with him, and they turn their backs on me as the principal drags me down the hall toward his office. She doesn't believe me. I can tell that she doesn't.

Why should she?

The truth is I've been avoiding Luna all day. I had to. It was best for all involved—definitely best for her. At least, that's what I kept chanting in my head all day. I almost convinced myself too.

But I needed to see her.

I thought I'd only go check on her. I'd see her from a distance and reassure myself she was okay, while getting a brief glance of her. That's all I was going to do. But, when I got here and saw Larry standing so close to her, watched as he reached out and grabbed her... *hurt her...* I couldn't stop myself. I can't ever seem to control myself when I'm around her. I never thought that staying away from her would be doing more harm than good.

Who would have started those tales?

It sure as hell wasn't me. When I look over my shoulder, I see my brother looking at me and see the victory in his eyes. There's my answer.

Fucking Atticus.

CHAPTER ELEVEN

LUNA

"Are you okay, Luna?" Atticus questions, and I don't bother answering. I'm not okay. I may never be okay again.

"Of course she's not okay, dumbass. Your brother has destroyed her," Jules snaps, pushing Atticus out of the way.

We're sitting outside on one of the concrete tables the school has placed around the back courtyard. We all congregate here every day for lunch and usually there's chatter and plenty of laughter. It's one of the best parts of my day. Now it is definitely one of the worst.

"It's going to be okay, Luna," Jules says, petting my hair trying to bring me comfort.

It doesn't work. She's lying. It will not be okay. There's no way that any of this will be okay ever again.

"This is all my fault."

My heart squeezes inside of my chest.

"It's not," I whisper, my voice sounding raw and painful.

"It is. I—"

"You aren't responsible for Gavin, Attie," I tell him, and it hurts just saying his name. I close my eyes against the force of that anguish.

"It's going to be okay," Jules insists stubbornly. "You were too good for the likes of Gavin Lodge. He doesn't deserve you," she says, hugging me and I let her. I put my forehead against hers and cry, taking whatever comfort my bestie can give me, but definitely feeling alone.

"This is my fault," Atticus says again, and I wish he'd just hush. I wish they'd all leave but Jules. She's the only one I want to see me when it feels like my world has imploded.

"You'll get through this, Luna."

Jules is right. I will get through this, but only because I don't have a choice.

"He did this because of me," Atticus mumbles. I force myself to look at him as Jules turns around to face him.

"What are you saying?" Jules asks and Atticus looks at me and I see grief and guilt written on his face. He's blaming himself and I hate that. This is all my fault, not his.

"Gavin knew I cared about Luna. He knew I..." he breaks off, looking uncomfortable.

"Attie, I don't—"

"He knew I had feelings for you, Luna. He knew it and he wanted to cause me pain. He always wants to cause me pain. My brother gets pleasure in hurting me. That's the kind of guy he is. He went after you because he knew that would hurt me like nothing else he could do."

Oh God.

Jules was right. There is competition between Gavin and Atticus, much more than I ever expected. That's the real reason Gavin finally decided to talk to me. That's why he invited me out to the dock. That's why once I was there that he didn't try to kiss me or feel me up. That explains everything. Gavin isn't attracted to me. I was only a tool to hurt his brother...

"I'm going to be sick," I cry, my hand going to my mouth. I jump up and take off running toward the building, praying I can make it to the bathroom before the bile rises up and forces itself out.

"Luna!" I hear Atticus yell, but I ignore him. I'm already the laughing stock of the school. The last thing I need is for everyone to see me losing my breakfast

Jules is beside me and she's shielding me as I sprint to the restroom. I slam through the doors and barely make it to the toilet in time.

My body heaves, ridding me of the contents of my stomach and only adding to my misery. I close my eyes and fall back on my ass when I'm done, feeling utterly humiliated and broken.

Jules brings a wet paper towel over, handing it to me and I use it to clean my mouth. She puts another one on my forehead and I let her, not because it's helping, but just because I don't have the will or strength to remove it.

"What am I going to do, Jules?" I whisper miserably, looking at my best friend.

"You're going to survive and make Gavin Lodge regret the day he ever tried to hurt you," she says solemnly.

"I never want to see him again," I tell her and even saying it, I know that I'm lying.

I'm so stupid.

I want Gavin to rush in and tell me it's all a mistake. I want him to tell me that he didn't tell the whole school that we slept together. I want him to tell me I wasn't just a girl he used to hurt his brother. I know it would be all lies, but I want those lies. I need them.

And I know that if Gavin gave them to me... I'd believe them.

I'm pathetic.

I don't know how long Jules and I sit in the restroom like that. Eventually, we get up and she goes to class. I can't bring myself to do that. It might be taking the coward's way out, but I go to the office and call my mom to come and get me. I can't be at school today. I can't pretend everything is okay when I feel like I'm dying.

I'll face it all tomorrow. Today I want to go home.

I sit in the secretary's office and wait for my mom to show up. We only live twenty minutes from the school and I know my mom left immediately. Still, those twenty minutes feel like a lifetime.

"You okay, baby?" Mom asks, rushing in the room. I look up at her to reassure her I'm fine—even if I'm not. But the minute I see her, I can't stop myself from going to her and letting her hug me. My tears start then, and I let them fall because I'm safe with my mom. She signs me out and we're finally leaving. Maybe once I get out of here, I will be able to breathe again.

"Luna."

My head jerks around and I see Gavin coming out of the principal's office. He looks upset, which is laughable. He's the cause of all of this.

I turn away from him. That's the only reply he deserves.

"Luna, we need to talk," Gavin says again.

I ignore him.

"Let's go, Mom," I whisper, just needing out of here.

"Who is that, Moonbeam?"

I normally hate it when Mom calls me her nickname in public. Today it's oddly comforting. I look over my shoulder at Gavin.

"No one, Mom. He's no one," I tell her and despite my soft voice, I can see that Gavin hears the words. It almost looks like he flinches and that should make me feel better, but it doesn't…

Not really.

I turn back to my mom and she may not completely understand, but I think she understands enough. She puts her arm around me and leads me out of the office and away from Gavin Lodge.

At least for today.

CHAPTER TWELVE

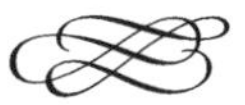

GAVIN

I watch as Luna practically runs in the opposite direction the minute that she sees me. It's been this way for a week. I should let it go. This is what I want. I need her to leave me alone. She has to be the one to leave me alone, because I'm not strong enough to be the one to walk away.

I hate that she thinks I'm the asshole who would spread lies about her. I hate that she believes I would tell anyone anything about the two of us. I want to prove to her I'm not, but I can't do that either.

It's better this way.

At least that's what I keep telling myself. I slide down against a tree, bring my legs up, and rest my hands on my knees. Then, I look at the table that she scurried off to and watch as Luna sits down with her friends.

Atticus isn't there.

He's home after I fucked him up. He's the one that told Larry I was bragging about sleeping with Luna. I'm sure he told others to. I wanted to leave him in a lot worse shape than I did. He's lucky he's only nursing sore ribs and a black eye. I was angry enough to leave him breathing through a straw.

Every now and then I can see Luna looking over at me. She knows I'm watching her, and I don't bother hiding the fact that I am. Truth be known, I can't tear my eyes away from her.

I don't know how one girl can be so damn beautiful, but she is. Today she's wearing her hair straight and it looks lighter as the sun shines down on it. She's the most beautiful thing I've ever laid my eyes on.

"I know that look."

I look over at Wally and frown. I like him. He's a good friend, but I'm definitely not in the mood for company.

"Don't know what you're talking about," I lie.

"Bullshit. If you stare at her any harder, she's going to call the cops on you."

"There's no laws about staring at someone."

"There is the way you're doing it, Gav. Damn, boy, if you liked the girl that much then why were you spreading shit all over the school about her. You know how girls are. They might like to get freaky under the sheets, but they sure as hell don't want you to spread that crap and ruin their good girl image. And, if there was ever a girl in the school that protects her image it would be Luna Marshall. Hell, I think until this happened the entire student body expected her to move into a nunnery after school."

"Just let it go, Wally. Nothing happened."

"Nothing?"

"Not a damn thing."

"Then, why in the hell did you say it did, Gav?"

I don't bother replying. I could tell him what a dick my brother is. I could deny everything, but there's no reason. People are going to believe what they want, and Atticus is the poster child of being everything I'm not. There's no way they'd believe he's behind all of this. Besides, I knew I was the one who went after Luna after knowing that Atticus was interested in her. In some ways, I probably deserve this shit.

Luna didn't, however.

I need to fix that.

"It doesn't matter. Just make sure it gets spread around school that I lied."

"Gav—"

"Just do it, Wally."

"Okay, if you can handle the fallout, it's no skin off my nose."

I shake my head.

I'm not important.

Only Luna...

CHAPTER THIRTEEN

LUNA

"Did you hear what Gavin Lodge did now?"

The mention of Gavin's name is enough to make my stomach hurt. It doesn't matter that it's been almost two weeks since that night on the docks. It all still feels like yesterday, especially the part where I found out he spread those tales around school.

"I don't really care," I lie. I do care and Jules probably knows that, but I don't have to admit to it. That's the beauty about having a best friend. You can lie and they'll pretend to believe you because they know that's what you need right now.

"He told Wally that he lied."

"He what?"

"Hand to God, Luna! He told Wally Andrews that he lied. That he didn't sleep with you and that you didn't even give him the time of day. Wally is telling everyone, including Motormouth Molly McKay and you know what that means."

"It'll be all over school by the end of the day," I mutter.

"Girl, it already is."

"Great," I say on a sigh, slamming my locker door shut.

"What? I thought this was what you wanted."

"No, what I wanted was for Gavin Lodge to disappear off the face of the earth."

"What you wanted was for him not to be an asshole," Jules corrects, and I stare up at the ceiling.

"Yeah, I guess so. But what he did isn't going to fix anything. Now instead of being the school slut, I'll just be back to being the icebox queen. I'm not sure which is better at this point."

"I see what you're saying."

"Why do you think he did it?"

"What? Lie? Who knows, Luna. Maybe he wanted a boost in popularity."

"No, why do you think he admitted the truth to Wally?"

"Wally is his best friend. I think he might be his only friend. Maybe he didn't think Wally would tell everyone in the school. Wally's kind of cute, don't you think?"

"Maybe, it just seems weird that he would lie about me and then turn around confessing the truth soon after," I mutter as we walk down the hall.

"I mean, he's got big ears, and I don't really dig guys with light colored hair, but he's not bad, right?"

"Gavin?"

"No, dummy. Wally Andrews."

"He's alright, I guess. I never really thought about it."

"I think he's cute. Course if we get married then I'll be stuck being called Julie Andrews and people will make fun of me and sing those weird musical numbers from *The Sound of Music.* That's a third level of hell that I don't need in my life."

"You've just turned seventeen, Jules. I don't think you need to worry about marriage just now."

"It never hurts for a girl to scope out her options, Luna. Maybe you ought to do the same."

"No thank you. I'm swearing off boys."

"Gavin Lodge is not the only hot guy in this world, Luna. There are plenty of other fish in the sea."

"They're all idiots, regardless," I mutter.

"You have options. That's all I'm saying," she reminds me as we make it into Mrs. Francis' AP English class.

I give her a look that I hope she interprets as 'no way in hell.' Then, I make my way back to my seat. My eyes automatically go across the room to the back row. Gavin Lodge is sitting there. He's wearing a faded red t-shirt and worn blue jeans. His hair is rumpled, and it looks like he forgot to brush it today. It looks really good.

He looks really good.

He's staring at me. I avoid his eyes and turn back around to look toward the front of the class.

I know I should hate him. Instead, all I feel is sad and broken. That's silly, I know.

It just doesn't change things.

CHAPTER FOURTEEN

GAVIN

en Months Later

"Happy Birthday."

Luna's head jerks up and when she looks at me all of the color leaves her face.

"My birthday was months ago," she mutters, turning away from me.

I reach out and grab her hand, even though I shouldn't. I shouldn't have spoken to her. I shouldn't have followed her out of the school. I shouldn't have, but I couldn't stop myself and here we are. Now, I'm touching her and reaching out to her, because I can't stop that either.

"Let me go, Gavin," she demands, and it might be my imagination, but her voice sounds like it's filled with anguish.

I hate like hell that I'm hurting her, but the last ten months have left me hollow inside. I kept thinking that time would make it easier, but it turns out, once you've had Luna Marshall in your arms, there's no going back.

At least not for me.

"Talk to me, Luna. Just for a minute."

"I don't think we have anything to say to each other."

She's right. Only I need to just the same.

"I just want to talk. Do you like being a senior?"

It's a lame question, but then again, everything I can come up with in my head sounds lame.

"What do you want, Gavin?"

"You look beautiful tonight."

Her face goes pale, I see it even with only the lights around the school and the moon. It was a stupid thing to say.

That's me.

Stupid and lame.

"I'll see you around," she says, moving to walk away, but her foot twists and she stumbles. I dive in, catching her quickly, before she falls from the concrete patio that we're on and tumbles down the steps. Her body goes stiff in my arms. I look down at her beautiful face and my heart squeezes inside of my chest.

Telling her she was beautiful might have been a stupid thing to say, but it was true. The school is having their back to school dance tonight and I didn't really come for it. I came to see Luna. She didn't bring a date, neither did her friend Jules. Jules hooked up at the dance, but except for a few dances—one with my worthless brother—Luna spent most of the night solo or with her friends. She was easily the prettiest girl there, wearing a soft teal silk dress and her long hair pulled up on top of her head. She changed her hair color over the summer. It's bright blonde now, getting rid of the soft golden hair from before. I like both. Then again, I'd like Luna even if she was bald. She's beautiful inside and out, it's simply that the outside is gorgeous too.

She straightens back up and pulls out of my arms. I let her go, because really, I have no choice.

"Thanks," she mumbles.

"Luna—"

"Gavin—"

I give a half-hearted smile. "You first."

"Why?"

"Luna—"

"Why did you do it? That's all I want to know. You had to know I liked you. Did you enjoy hurting me? Was it really just a way to get even with Attie?"

"What's between us, Luna—"

"There's nothing really between us," she argues and she's wrong.

"What's between us has nothing to do with Atticus, Luna."

"I wish I could believe you."

"Would it be too much to start over, Luna?"

"We never really started to begin with. Besides, what do you care? Aren't you leaving after graduation?"

"Well, yeah."

"And I'm not."

"You'll be going to college."

"A community college. I don't really want to leave Stone Lake, Gavin. I never have. I don't have a reason to."

It's on the tip of my tongue to ask her to let me be the reason. *God.* What would it be like to have Luna in my corner, to have her with me when I leave here? What would it be like knowing that everything I do, I'm doing for her? I could make her happy, I know I could.

This past ten months without having contact with her, have been hell. Watching her from a distance, seeing her in town and hiding so she didn't think I was stalking her—which I was—all while knowing what it felt like to hold her in my arms, to have her smiles and laughter—if only for one night—has nearly destroyed me. Watching Atticus still being in her life, after the pain he caused her, was worse.

"There's a whole school year between now and then, maybe we could start over," I tell her, laying it out and those words feel like they're torn out of my chest, but if anyone deserves honesty from me, deserves to have me expose how I really feel, it's Luna.

"I don't understand."

"I want you in my life, Luna."

"You didn't before."

"I did. There are things that you don't understand, and I'll tell you, one day. For now, I'm asking you to give me a chance to prove that I might be an asshole, but I'm not the kind of one you think I am."

"That literally makes zero sense," she says, studying my face closely. I let her, knowing that I'll never get another chance. This is it.

All or nothing.

"I want time with you, Luna. That's about as much sense as I can make. That's all I got."

"I..."

My heart kicks in my chest. I don't know why, but she's weakening. I see it in her face. I hear it in her voice. My mouth goes dry, because I know that this is one of the most important moments in my life.

"I've wanted to ask you to dance with me all night, Luna. Will you dance with me now?" I ask her, holding out my hand.

"There's no music." Her voice is so soft it feels like she's touching me.

"We can make our own," I tell her, and it feels like I'm holding my breath as she slowly puts her hand in mine and I pull her into me, wrapping my arms around her.

We sway against the backdrop of crickets and other sounds of the night, and I can't remember a thing in my life that has felt as special.

CHAPTER FIFTEEN

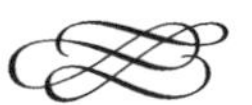

LUNA

You can call me crazy. That's nothing compared to the names I'm calling myself. After what he did, the last thing I should do is give Gavin Lodge the time of day. I can't explain why I am. If I'm honest, it's because I want to. The night we shared out on the dock has haunted me. It's haunted me because I think that night, I got a glimpse of the real Gavin. The side he doesn't let anyone see. Maybe I'm fooling myself, and completely wrong. Maybe I'm even lying to myself because I want Gavin to be the person I've always imagined and dreamed he was.

Maybe I'm a fool.

The only thing I know for sure is that I've been miserable since the day Gavin and Larry got into that fight. Pushing all thoughts of Gavin from my mind has failed to work, too. There's one other thing that I know. As I lay my head against Gavin's chest, hear his heart beating in my ear, and feel his arms close around me, I know that this is where I am meant to be.

This is it.

Gavin is the one I've been waiting my whole life for.

"Damn," he hisses. His voice is raw and gravely and hearing it, goosebumps spread over my skin.

"What is it?"

"I just never thought I'd have you in my arms again, Luna, and I can't tell you how much that thought has hurt me."

"I didn't think anything about me could hurt you, Gavin."

He pulls back and looks down at me. His hand slides against the side of my neck and his thumb comes up and brushes along my jawline as he studies me. I don't know what he's thinking, but I know there's something going on in his head. I wish I could read him better to know.

"I have a feeling Luna Marshall, you can hurt me more than anyone."

"I would never hurt you, Gavin. Never," I vow, because I wouldn't. I couldn't. I'm not that kind of person, but more than that Gavin is special to me. I never want to hurt him.

I stare up at him, wanting him to believe me. My heart stutters in my chest. Whatever is going on here, it *feels* important.

He closes his eyes and drops his head down so that it rests on mine. His arms tighten around me, and I figure if a person could die from happiness I might right now. I might be a fool, and I'm pretty sure Jules will be the first one to tell me that, but I don't think I care. Right now, all that matters is Gavin and how he makes me feel.

"Why does your mom call you Moonbeam?"

"You heard that," I whisper, smiling as we move together, and I settle my head back against his chest.

"Yeah."

"That's embarrassing," I admit, and I can feel myself blushing.

"It's sweet. I liked it."

"When I was little, I used to beg her to read to me and my favorite book was *Goodnight Moon.* When I was sick, hearing Mom read that to me always made me feel better, no matter what."

"*Goodnight Moon?*"

"It's this silly children's book, but I just loved the way Mom sounded when she read it to me. It always made me feel… safe."

"That's good to have," he says, and his voice sounds funny. I remember what Atticus said about his father, and I can't imagine the way that Gavin and Attie were forced to grow up. I squeeze Gavin a little tighter. I don't say anything, because I know he wouldn't want my pity and that's not what it is really. I only hate that he has such a hard time. I hate that's what his life is like at home. It has to hurt him. Maybe after what he did to me, I shouldn't feel for him… *but I do.*

"It is. Anyways when I was like ten, Mom had a breast cancer scare," I confide in him, understating what actually happened. "I actually don't talk or remember a lot about it. I don't like to think of my mother as sick. I can't imagine a world without her in it."

"I get that."

"One day I came home from school early and Mom wasn't waiting on the porch like she normally did. I found her in her bedroom, lying on the bed crying. She was holding this large lock of her hair." My voice catches as I relive the memory. It's been years, but I can still see the vision of my mom holding her hair like that and crying as if it were yesterday.

"Damn, Baby," he murmurs into my hair and despite my sadness, I smile.

"I went into my room, grabbed the book off my shelf, and I took it in there to read the story to her because I wanted her to feel safe too. When I told her why, she said it did make her feel better. Mom said I was her very own personal moonbeam. It just kind of stuck after that."

Gavin doesn't say anything and I'm starting to feel self-conscious, when he pulls back and looks at me.

"I've never met anyone like you in my life," he whispers and before I know what to say or how to react, he bends down, and he kisses me.

My very first kiss.

I don't know what I expected. You build fantasies up in your mind and you plan for them to be perfect. I'm old enough to know that things never live up to your expectations. But, this kiss does. It's awkward but sweet at first. I have no idea what I'm doing and I let him lead me. His tongue seeks mine out and slides against it. Shyly, I imitate the same movement, not wanting to disappoint him. There's a scent to our kiss, an aroma that I wasn't expecting. I thought kisses would be about touching and feeling. While it is, it's also more. There's an earthy scent that feels just a little wicked and as I moan into his mouth the kiss deepens. Those feelings of desire multiply and my body feels as if it's floating in pleasure. It's surreal that my first kiss was with Gavin Lodge. I'd given up that dream, but it happened and…

It was perfect.

CHAPTER SIXTEEN

GAVIN

"Hey."

"Gavin," Luna purrs my name into the phone, and I hear the pleasure in her voice. She likes that I called, and she doesn't try to hide it. That does something to me that I can't explain, I just know I like it. Luna's the first person in my life who has wanted me around. The first person to make me feel like I matter.

"Hey, Moonbeam," I respond, and I can hear her giggle and it makes me smile.

"I didn't think you'd call me."

"I told you I was going to make sure you made it home okay."

"I know, but you didn't have to."

"I wanted to. Thanks for dancing with me tonight," I tell her, and she has no idea how much the memory of her in my arms means to me.

"I had fun," she responds, and I can almost hear the smile in her voice.

"I was wondering if maybe you'd like to go with me tomorrow to the dock? We could meet and..."

"The dock?"

"Yeah. Do you fish?"

"Well, duh," she laughs.

"So, what do you think?"

"Where do I meet you? I don't drive yet. I need to, but Dad's working all the time and Mom gets nervous. Jules said she'd teach me, but... Have you seen her drive?"

"Yeah, Babe. I can teach you if you want."

"You will?"

"Definitely."

"I'd really like that, Gavin."

"We'll start tomorrow," I promise, deciding as long as she's happy that I'd agree to almost anything.

"I can't believe you'd do that."

"Do you think your girl will cover for you?"

"Jules?"

"Yeah. Do you think she'd agree to cover for you with your parents?"

"I'm sure she would, but she doesn't have to. My parents will be fine if I tell them I'm going out with you. They will probably just want to meet you first."

I ignore the panic that makes me feel. I know that Luna thinks her parents will welcome me with open arms. She doesn't see me as less, but I know without even thinking about it that her parents will for sure.

"How about we keep the fact that we're dating just between us right now?" I suggest, hating that I do it, but feeling like I need to, all the same.

"But... are we dating, Gavin?"

"Yeah. I just... I don't want anyone to know, until I can prove that I deserve you, Luna."

"Gavin, you don't need—"

"You don't trust me. You can't deny that. A couple hours of us dancing and talking to each other, hasn't erased six months for you."

"I just don't understand why you told—"

"I didn't tell them anything, Luna."

"But everyone was talking about it and even your friend Wally—"

"I know you don't have a reason to believe me, Luna, but I didn't say anything."

"Then, who did?"

I take an aggravated breath. I don't know how to answer that. If I tell her the truth, I don't think she'd believe me. She's friends with Atticus, she hasn't seen how he really is. She has no idea the kind of bastard he can be.

"I'm not sure," I lie.

Luna remains silent and I'm scared that I'm losing my shot and I don't want that. Luna cares for me and she definitely deserves better.

But the simple truth is, I want her.

"Just give me a chance, Luna. No one but us will know we're even talking to each other. Give me a chance to prove to you that you can trust me."

It seems like forever before she answers and each passing second is painful.

"Pick me up at Jules' house around one tomorrow. Is that okay?"

"It's perfect. I can't wait to see you again, Moonbeam."

"That's a silly nickname," she gripes but I can hear the humor behind her complaint.

"It fits you. I'll see you tomorrow, Baby."

"See you tomorrow, Gavin."

I hold the phone until she hangs up, and I don't even realize right then that I'm smiling.

But I am.

CHAPTER SEVENTEEN

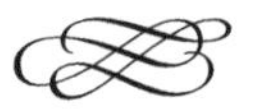

LUNA

"I can't believe you're agreeing to meet that dick-weed," Jules huffs.

"Jules, I like him."

"*Luna,* he hurt you. Please tell me you haven't forgotten that."

"I haven't, but he says he didn't do it."

"Bullshit. If it wasn't him then who else would it have been?"

"I don't know, but he really seemed sincere, Jules."

"You're just blinded. I don't like this Luna. I don't like it at all."

I frown. We're sitting on the steps of her front porch waiting for Gavin. I'm wearing a pair of cut offs and my favorite pink tank. I've got my bikini on underneath. I don't know if I'll need it, but I thought it was better to be safe than sorry. Jules is definitely not happy that I'm meeting Gavin, but that was to be expected. Not many people know how truly hurt I was by Gavin. I didn't let anyone see except Jules. Mom knew I was hurt, she didn't know the details and I didn't volunteer them. But, for the most part, I kept my pain to myself.

Jules is my best friend and no matter what we have each other's backs. That's the rule and I'm grateful—even if right now it's annoying.

"So noted."

"Bitch," she mutters, smiling at me and I smile back at her.

"Jules?"

"What?" she snaps, clearly telling me she's still upset.

"I really, *really* like Gavin."

"Luna, you think lions are pretty too, but you still wouldn't get in a cage with one."

"I don't think Gavin wants to eat me alive, Jules."

"He'll break your heart again."

"Jules—"

"And then I'll have to kill him, which means I'll go to jail and even though my parents kind of think that is going to happen anyway, it will break their hearts and I'll have to go potty in a cell with other women and *that* will break my heart. Not to mention I won't be able to wear makeup and—"

"You might meet a hot cop and you know how you dig men in uniform," I joke.

"Quit trying to give me reasons to end Gavin Lodge's miserable life," she complains while smiling at me.

"Jules, if Heath Ledger were to show up on our doorstep right now and ask you out and you could see in the future and know that going out with him means you are going to die a horrible death and you have to decide if going out with him is worth it. Would you still go?"

"How horrible are we talking?" she hedges.

"He sends you a breakup text while you're driving down the road behind a truck carrying a load of steel pipes and you're so distraught you don't notice they aren't secured properly. You look up right in time to see a steel pipe break free, crash through your windshield and impale you right through the neck, severing your head from your body in *Final Destination* style."

"Did we have sex before I died?"

"You had sex."

"Damn it. I'd still go out with him."

"And that's how I feel about Gavin."

She lets out a long drawn out sigh, and I expect her to give me more flack about it when we hear a vehicle pull into her drive. I look up to see Gavin's old beat-up truck pull into the driveway.

"Speak of the devil," Jules grumbles.

"Be nice."

"I'm always nice," she lies, but it makes me laugh.

We stand up and I start walking to Gavin's truck, Jules following me. I get to it just as he opens the door and steps out. I don't give myself time to think about it. Instead, I go straight to him, hugging him close. This happiness fills me from seeing him again. There's a part of me that was afraid I dreamed yesterday up in my head and it didn't really happen. My eyes close as Gavin's arms come around me and he holds me even closer. When I pull away, he's grinning down at me, and I feel warm and flushed all over.

"Hey, Jules."

"Gavin," Jules utters rudely, proving she's going to be a hard ass about this. I give her a warning look, but she ignores me.

"You ready, Babe?" Gavin asks.

"I'm ready."

"You got your permit with you?"

"Permit?"

"To drive, Moonbeam," he laughs.

"Oh. Yeah."

"Good. Then, hop in."

"I... You want me to drive your truck?" I squeak.

"I told you I'd teach you to drive, remember?"

"I thought you meant, you know have me watch you and take notes or something."

"Best way to learn is to do it, Luna," he says, opening his door.

"I... if you're sure," I concede, praying I don't wreck and destroy his truck.

Gavin keeps his hand on the small of my back and ushers me

inside the truck. Then, he helps lift me up in the big tall monstrosity. I'm still recovering from the feel of his hands on me when he leans down to buckle me in.

"Got to keep my girl safe," he whispers and kisses my lips in a light peck.

I'm pretty sure I turn into a puddle of goo and my bones all completely melt. My eyes go to Jules and she's looking at me with surprise.

"Moonbeam?"

She mouths the word, not letting sound escape, but I know what she says and I just grin. She shakes her head then turns her attention to Gavin. He's walking around the front of the truck and Jules falls in behind him. He gets inside and Jules grabs his door before he can shut it.

"I don't trust you, Gavin Lodge," she warns.

"Jules—"

"I can understand that," Gavin says, interrupting me.

"If you hurt Luna again, there won't be anyone or anything that can save you from me."

"Okay," he replies, studying her. I hold my head down on the steering wheel, banging it slightly.

"I'm serious. You hurt her again and I don't care if it means I'm decapitated before I have the chance to have Heath Ledger's beautiful babies. I don't even care if it means my head is torn from my body, thrown into the swamp, and becomes a midnight snack to a nest of crocodiles, I will hurt you."

"Uh... So noted, Jules."

"Good. As long as we got that clear. You two have fun now," she singsongs, slamming his door a little too hard.

"Uh... Gavin..." I start, wondering how to explain Jules.

"Put her in neutral, Moonbeam and start it up."

"About Jules..."

"She's fine. Let's get moving. We have fish to catch."

"She's just..."

"She's looking out for you, Luna. That's a good thing."

"Yeah," I whisper wearing a smile, because he's grinning at me and his finger is moving along the side of my face.

"You ready to drive?"

"Umm... just one question."

"What's that?"

"What do you mean put it in neutral?" I ask.

"Oh boy," he chuckles, and I blush, because I wasn't really kidding. Mom's car has a gearshift that's easy to understand. Gavin's truck is a standard, and I can't remember ever being in a vehicle that wasn't automatic. I'm completely lost. But I figure as long as I get to hear Gavin laughing, I don't really care if I do make a complete fool of myself.

It's worth it.

CHAPTER EIGHTEEN

GAVIN

"How did I do?" Luna asks, her face flushed. She blows her bangs out of her face, looking so proud that I don't have the heart to tell her the truth.

My clutch and transmission are glad we finally made it to the lake.

"You did really good, Moonbeam."

"Really?" she cries excitedly, her hand slapping in victory against the steering wheel.

"I thought it was getting better there as we turned to the old lake. I didn't even stall at the stop sign but once."

"Yep, that's better than I did my first time," I lie.

"Yay! I might really get the hang of this Gavin."

"Yeah, you might," I laugh. "Are you ready to go sink some worms?"

Her nose scrunches up on her face and it makes me want to laugh. "Do you have to say it like that?"

I lean down and kiss her lips again, just another brief peck, giving me a small taste of her. Her lips part against mine, but I resist tasting her deeper for now. I'm definitely not a saint, but Luna is special, and I want her to know that.

"Let's go fishing," I murmur, and she looks at me smiling so intently that it seems to light up everything around us.

"Sounds good."

I grab the poles and tackle box, while Luna gets the small cooler that she brought, and we walk hand in hand toward the dock. Being here with her again feels right. Memories of the night we shared, of her lying in my arms all come rushing back to me, so strong that it's almost as if they have a taste and it's definitely sweet.

We settle down in silence. Merely passing small talk here and there as I bait her hook followed with mine. We sit on the edge of the dock, feet dangling off, Luna barefoot. It might be the single best time of my life. Maybe even better than the night we slept out here, because my brother isn't close by. He has no idea I'm here and he won't for as long as I can keep him in the dark. I don't want him to taint what Luna and I have. If he hurts her again, I'll kill him, and I'm not just saying that. Whatever ties we shared aren't even a memory. I can't change that. I don't even want to. I don't know what it says about me, but I hate my brother.

"You got quiet," Luna observes. She puts her hands over her eyes like a visor as she looks at me, to guard them from the sun.

"I was just thinking."

"What about?"

I start to lie, but I don't want to—not with Luna and not about this.

"About Atticus."

"Your brother?" she asks, sounding confused, and maybe a little surprised.

"I don't want him to know about us, Luna."

"Uh…"

"At least for now. I want time for whatever is between us, just to be about the two of us."

"You keep saying that. I'm starting to feel like some dirty little secret you want to keep, Gavin."

"Now you're talking insane. You're the prettiest girl in school… What?" I stop and ask when she scrunches her nose up and looks unhappy.

"No girl wants to be called the prettiest girl in school."

"But, Babe, you are," I laugh as her expression gets more frustrated. "Quit being cute."

"Cute and pretty. It's like you hate me," she whines.

I full out laugh. I can't stop. Luna makes me feel free and that's a sensation I've never had in my life.

"Babe." I shake my head, still unable to control my laughter.

"Can't I be gorgeous? Beautiful? Sexy? Dangerous? Geez!"

I put my fishing pole down and pull Luna in close. I stare into her eyes. The green in them shimmers like emeralds. She's not wearing makeup like most of the girls at school do. Luna doesn't need it. I drop my head down to hers, eyes wide open, keeping my gaze focused, and making sure she can see the truth in what I'm telling her.

"You're so beautiful you take my breath away."

"Gavin…" she murmurs, her voice soft and sweet. It wraps around me, slides inside of me. I love the way she says my name. I love the tender look on her face as she does. Jesus, I like everything about Luna Marshall. I kiss her, hoping that she can feel what she does to me, hoping to make her understand what she makes me feel.

I'm not sure I succeed, but it's a damn good kiss. It's the kind that erases the memory of any that came before it and probably any that might come after it. In my heart, I know, if I could only kiss Luna Marshall for the rest of my life, I'd die a happy man. I don't care if I am only eighteen.

It's completely true.

CHAPTER NINETEEN

LUNA

"Did you have a good birthday?"

I look up, surprised at Gavin's question.

"You're preoccupied with an event that has passed, Gavin."

"Humor me," he mumbles.

"It was okay. Dad was out of town for business, so Mom and I had lunch in town complete with cupcakes."

"That doesn't sound great. I figured you'd have a party."

"Nah," I respond. I don't tell him that things are tense at home lately. Something is going on with my parents, but when I ask them about it, they tell me I'm imagining things. "Let's stop talking about it. My birthday was lame. I enjoyed dancing with you much more."

"I think so too." He smirks and for some reason I really like that look on his face.

"I think all the fish are dead," I grumble, deciding to change the subject before I do something horribly stupid and blurt out that I love him. I mean I don't. How could I? We barely know each other and until our dance, we hadn't spoken in forever. It'd be crazy to love him…

Crazy.

I lay my pole down and lay back on the dock, looking up at the sky. The sun has moved, so it's not shining straight down on us now and I'm definitely glad for that.

"You'll lose your pole if a fish gets on it," he warns, but he's smiling down at me and he's got this lazy look on his face that makes me feel warm all over.

"Gavin, there are no fish in this lake."

"There are."

"Tell that to the poor worm you sank hours ago and has been suffering on the hook."

"It probably drowned, Babe."

"Worms can breathe underwater."

"Did I miss that fact in biology class or something?"

"When you take the worm out of the water, he's always squiggling."

"That doesn't mean he's alive," he counters.

My brows knit together. "Of course it does. Why else would he be *moving*?"

"Babe, things like that move after they die. Their bodies twitch from pain."

"Ew... They do not!"

"Babe, they do."

"You're just trying to gross me out!"

"I'm being honest. Haven't you seen a snake move after it's dead."

"Um... No. No, I haven't. You know, Gavin, if this is the way you talk to the girls at our school, it's a good thing you're hot, cause if not, your reputation would be a lot different." I close my eyes as I giggle, so I don't see what he's doing. All at once though I feel his hand on my stomach and as I jerk and look at him, I'm surprised to find him lying beside me.

"I'm teaching you here, Luna. You should pay attention."

"What are you teaching me?" I ask, suddenly left breathless.

"That some things make your body react out of your control," he responds. His eyes are intense and his hand on my stomach feels hot through my thin shirt. My heart is beating hard in my chest. I use my tongue to moisten my lips, rubbing them together nervously, because my mouth is suddenly dry.

"What things?" I whisper, hoping I'm tempting him. For the first time in my life, I want to tempt a boy. I want Gavin to lose control. I want him to lose control with me. I want his touch, his kiss and maybe more.

"Luna—"

"What things, Gavin?" I ask again. My voice is so hoarse, full of hunger for things I don't truly understand, that I barely recognize the desire.

"Damn," he growls, his lips close to mine, and then he kisses me.

His tongue slides into my mouth like a soldier intent on owning me. The ferociousness behind the sensual act would scare me if I didn't want him so much. I've never noticed before that kisses have tastes. There's the minty freshness of his mouth as if he had gum or candy, but there's something else, a deeper taste that feeds my growing hunger. Our tongues slide against one another, and I lose myself in the kiss, letting my worries fade and letting Gavin take control, allowing him to lead me where we need to go.

I feel his hand slide under my shirt and move across my stomach. I moan and Gavin swallows the sound. My hips rock and I clench the muscles in my body because it feels like there's a fire inside of me that has been fanned and is on the verge of becoming a wild blaze. His fingers skirt under my bikini top, as his thumb brushes against the swell of my breast.

This is it. This is what I've waited my whole life to experience. *These sensations*—the ones only Gavin awakens—are what Jules is always talking about, that I never understood.

"God, Luna," Gavin growls, when he breaks away for just a moment.

My eyes open slowly as I stare up at him. I've wanted this for so long, I feel like I might be in the middle of a dream. I lick my lips, and I can still taste him there. His gaze zeros in on my tongue and becomes so heated that I feel like it's burning me.

"Gavin, I—" I break off with a gasp, as at this exact moment, the moment when I'm foolishly about to tell him about how long I've wanted him to notice me, how often I think about him, want to talk to him, want to kiss him and definitely more... My fishing rod goes crazy. The reel lets out a buzzing noise as the line is being pulled at really quick speed. I stare in disbelief as the rod starts sliding down the dock.

Gavin must be as shocked as I am, because he doesn't reach over and grab the pole either. Actually, we both kind of stare at the rod not sure what's happening when all at once it makes a plopping noise as it falls into the water.

"Shit," Gavin mutters.

"We have to get it."

"Babe—"

"It's your fishing rod, Gavin."

"It's not that important."

"It is. You brought it for me to use and we have to get it."

"Babe the reel is—"

"I'll get it," I volunteer, feeling guilty, because I did put it down. In my defense I didn't think a giant killer fish would attack while I was otherwise occupied. My face flushes as I remember what Gavin and I were doing only moments earlier. I swear I can still feel his hand under my breast, and I miss the feel of it.

"Babe you don't have to—"

"I said I'll get it."

I stand and slide my cut offs down my legs, stepping out of them and tossing them to the side with my flip flops. Then I yank my shirt off and let it join them.

"Babe, you don't have to jump in the water. I won't say no to you standing there the rest of the day modeling that bikini though," Gavin says.

I look at him in surprise then smile because apparently, he likes my plain white bikini. I guess obsessing over if I should have worn something sexier was worrying over nothing.

"You could get in the water with me," I suggest.

"I like the idea of watching you model for me more."

I roll my eyes, looking heavenward. "Whatever," I mutter, shaking my head. "I mean if you're scared to get in the water, I guess it's up to me to save the day," I tease. Then, I jump into the water. I look back at the dock to see Gavin laughing. He's taking off his shoes, socks, and shirt. He keeps his jeans on, which is disappointing, but he jumps in. I start sputtering because his splashing into the water nearly drowns me. I wipe the water off my face all over again, kicking my legs to stay afloat.

"You're going to be a handful, Luna Marshall," he drones when he gets in front of me and then, he's kissing me again.

Maybe I should worry, but it sounds like Gavin likes me just the way I am, so instead, I kiss him until we slide under the water and kick back to the surface again.

CHAPTER TWENTY

GAVIN

"You haven't been around the house much on the weekends. I thought you were working, but you weren't at the grocery store today. Where have you been?"

I ignore the urge to hit my brother and tell him that it's not any of his business where I'm at.

"I didn't realize that you had such an unhealthy fascination with my life, Atticus."

"Just wondering what you're up to," he deflects, flopping on his bed.

I'm sure he'd like to know, but I'm not about to tell him—at least not right now. I want to keep it to myself for as long as I can. Luna and I have officially been seeing each other for three months now. Almost all of my weekends I spend with her and occasionally we get Wednesday nights together for a couple of hours. Even so, that's not enough time. I want to spend every waking moment with her. I've never felt like this before. I knew Luna Marshall was dangerous, but I don't think I appreciated how deeply I would become addicted to her.

And I'm definitely addicted.

"Not up to nothing, just school and work. I get some time off the last thing I want to do is come back here, so I find other places to be."

It's the truth, but not. Hopefully it's enough to satisfy him. I don't really give a damn, but I'd rather not have him snooping around Luna and me. Not right now. Things are going too good right now to have my asshole brother get involved and fuck it up.

"There are rumors going around at school that you're seeing a girl."

"Don't you have enough to worry about in your own life, Atticus? Do you have to be obsessed with mine?"

"I'm not obsessed with you."

"It sure as hell feels like it. Do me a favor and worry about your own shit and stay out of mine."

"No worries. You're always talking about leaving this place. You should just leave now. No one wants you around."

I ignore him. Instead of smarting off, I close my eyes and immediately Luna's smiling face comes to mind. Memories of the last kiss we shared, of touching her, hearing her moan my name. It's all right there, and she fills me as nothing else has in my life. I love her. I haven't told her, but the feelings are there. She has to know she's special. I hate not letting the world see that this beautiful woman cares about me, that she *belongs* to me. I want to shout it from the rooftops. I want the world to know that she chose me and that she thinks I'm worthy of her, even if no one else does.

It's hard to keep it a secret, so that's coming soon. Especially with all the boys circling around Luna. She shoots them down, but that doesn't mean I like sitting back and watching.

Things will change, though. I look over at Atticus, as if by instinct. I worry what will happen when they do. I can't help but worry because inside I know that my own brother will do everything that he can to destroy this for me. I think I can contain him, because I'm prepared for his lies now. I wasn't expecting them before, and he blindsided me. He won't get that chance again. So, yeah, I think I can handle him.

I'm not so sure about Luna's parents...

CHAPTER TWENTY ONE

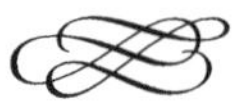

ATTICUS

"Let's go out."

I'm so damn nervous. My palms are sweating. I hope I don't sound desperate, but I feel like I am—Luna's forcing me to be. She keeps ignoring me, treating me as a buddy. It's driving me crazy. I can get any girl in this school and the one I want insists on seeing me as a friend. Sometimes I think she may pet me on the head and whisper, "Good boy."

This is Gavin's fault, of course. If he hadn't gotten Luna's hopes up things would have been different. I was making progress until then. He doesn't even like her. He just spent the night with her because he knew it would hurt me. I spied on them all night. Spending the night in the dark and listening to them. I always knew my brother was lame, but the fact that he could have fucked Luna and didn't proved it. I'm glad though. It would have changed everything. I don't want my brother's leftovers. I knew Luna was still a virgin. I knew exactly what happened between her and my brother, but I still spread the rumors at school about them. I still made sure it sounded like Gavin was the one who told me. I thought once Luna saw what a jerk my brother truly was, the realization would make her turn to me. It hasn't. It appears I'm going to have to do something drastic to get Luna's attention.

Why can't anything ever be easy?

"What?"

The surprise and almost panic in Luna's voice pisses me off, but I do my best to hide it.

"Go out with me. We could go watch the new scary movie."

"What movie?"

"The Hills Have Eyes."

"Ew. No, Attie. That movie looks gross. I don't like horror movies," Luna says, shaking her head. Frustration doesn't begin to describe what I'm feeling.

"What about scary movies?"

I look up as Jules walks over to us. *Great, just great*. I can't even get time alone with Luna. Something is going to have to change and soon.

"Attie wants us all to go watch that creepy movie that's coming out. Remember we saw it advertised the other night?"

"Oh, that one about the people that are stalked by monsters living in the desert? Uber creepy, Atticus. I don't need any more creepiness in my life. I've got too much as it is."

I bite back the retort that I didn't actually *invite* her to the movies. That would probably upset Luna.

Jules.

She grates on my nerves like a fly buzzing around that won't leave you alone. I don't know why Luna insists on being her friend.

"It doesn't have to be that movie," I mumble.

"I think I'm done with scary movies in general. They lose something after you get weird notes in your locker," Jules responds.

"Oh man, did you get another one?" Luna questions.

"Not a note this time, but a flower."

"I thought girls liked flowers?" I argue, figuring the rest of our lunch hour will be all about Jules and her stalker that's been putting notes and things in her locker. If you ask me, the bitch should be glad some guy is interested in her.

"Not like this," she mutters and reaches into the backpack she's carrying and pulls out a black rose.

Luna gasps.

I didn't think it was that bad, but I make a note never to buy her black roses.

If we ever get to that point of our relationship.

Something is going to have to change…

"Oh my God. Jules you have to tell your parents. That's just too much. It's almost… *threatening.*"

"Nah. Maybe whoever it is, is heavy into goth."

"You mean like that Bixler kid?"

"Ew. He's only a freshman. That'd ruin me."

"Or maybe that Laney chick that recently transferred here," I suggest with a smirk.

"A girl? Hmm… I never thought of that. I mean, I don't really think of girls that way."

"No muff diving for you?"

"Gross Atticus, do you have to call it that?" Luna says, scrunching up her nose.

She really is too innocent. I'll have to work to get her the way I want her. If I can ever get in there with her.

I shrug in reply.

"Still, she's kind of pretty in a Jennifer Love-Hewitt meets Jessica Alba and throw in Sarah Jessica Parker, just because."

"Because, why?" Luna asks.

"Because no one should be as pretty as Jennifer and Jessica. It defies the natural order of things." Jules lifts a shoulder.

"Luna's that pretty," I add in.

"Awe, Attie!" Luna laughs, blushing prettily.

"Yeah, awe, Attie. You really need to quit trying so hard. You're being your own kind of creepy," Jules mocks.

"I'm just stating the truth." I try not to growl the words at her.

"Desperate, much?" Jules whispers, rolling her eyes at me.

"Jules, leave Atticus alone. He doesn't mean anything like that. He knows we're just friends."

"But does he, Luna?"

"Of course he does. Right, Attie?"

"Right," I mutter, unable to say much more.

"And that's all you'll ever be," Jules says, her eyes mocking me and as usual, Luna is clueless.

"Attie is one of my best friends. I'd be lost without either of you," Luna argues. "Right now, though, I better get. I have to meet Mrs. Raine in the library for a makeup biology exam. I missed it the other day when I went to the dentist. Catch you guys on the flipside," she calls over her shoulder, walking away.

"Don't you ever get tired of sporting a hard on for Luna, knowing she'll never think of you as more than a pet?" Jules asks me.

"You don't know what you're talking about."

"I know my girl would rather kiss anyone at this school than you, and that includes yours truly."

"Whatever. Luna doesn't see me as anyone other than her friend yet. She will."

"When pigs fly. Hate to break it to you, Attie, but you've been friend-zoned for life when it comes to Luna."

"I don't—"

"Even if by some miracle. I mean, let's say lightning came down from the gods and struck Luna and she suddenly realized that you're madly in love with her, there's no way she'd ever go there with you."

"Why not? Lots of girls in this school want me."

"Of course they do, you're hot. You got that unrequited love thing going and you rock it. Luna only sees you as Gavin's little brother. You're doomed with her."

"You're wrong. Gavin and Luna are over. She wants nothing to do with my brother, not since he spread those lies on her. She's done with him."

"Oh poor, poor Atticus. You're so blind to how girls really think."

"I don't think so," I grumble.

Jules slides next to me. We're both sitting on the ground, under the shade of an old Maple tree. She reaches up and slides her fingers in my hair and she bites her lip. I know what she wants. You'd have to be stupid not to. Jules isn't like Luna. She's not innocent. I've never gone there with her, because of Luna, but most of the boys in our class have. I look down at her chest. Her light pink shirt has a wide V-neck and it's open to show a lot of cleavage. You can see the black silk strap of her bra and the dark color bleeds through under the shirt, so that you can see the form of her breasts perfectly.

"Don't you get tired of pining over a girl who will never see you as a man, Attie? Who will never give you the pleasure you deserve? Who will always prefer your brother over you?"

"What do you know that I don't?"

"Exactly what I'm telling you. But don't worry, Attie. I'm here to heal your wounded heart, and I'll kiss it all better."

"You will, huh?"

"Definitely."

"You can't ever tell, Luna."

"It will be our secret," she agrees with a smile as I move my hand up to squeeze her tit. "Our dirty little secret."

She's not the one I want, but she might prove useful and a guy can't live on love alone. I shrug, standing up. Jules gets up too and I let her lead me. I know she's headed to the weight lifting room. The showers in the back are legendary around here.

Looks like Jules and I will be missing fifth period.

CHAPTER TWENTY TWO

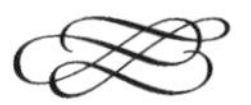

LUNA

It's official. Maine's weather is on crack. A few weeks back we could sit outside with our coats on and have lunch. Today it's snowing and school has been canceled. There's so much snow that it will take weeks to dig out. The white stuff might be beautiful, but I'm definitely not a fan. I won't get to spend this weekend with Gavin and the thought of going so long without seeing him or being around him hurts me.

"You look awful sad today, Moonbeam."

"Just sick of the white stuff outside."

"One of the pleasures of living in Maine," Mom laughs and she's not wrong.

"What are you doing?" I ask her, deciding to change the subject because there's not much I can do about the weather. I can't invite Gavin over either, because if he got hurt on these roads, I'd never forgive myself.

"Going over my shopping list for Thanksgiving dinner."

"Will Daddy be here?"

"Of course he will, Luna. It's Thanksgiving. Where else would he be?"

"I don't know, he seems to be out of town a lot lately."

"It's only travel for work. It will get better."

"I hope so, I miss him," I tell her, and I do, but I'm more worried about Mom. I hear her crying at night when she thinks I'm asleep. There's something going on, and I know that she's trying to shield me from it.

"Are Gramma and Pop-pop coming in this year?"

"They can't make it this time, Moonbeam. Mom is still having trouble with her hip, but we'll go visit them soon."

"Good, I miss them."

"Me too."

"Umm... Mom..." I ask, wringing my hands nervously in my lap.

"Do you think I could ask someone to come eat dinner with us?"

"Jules? Won't she be eating with her family?"

"I think they're going to Florida."

"Now I'm jealous," Mom jokes.

"Yeah, me too," I laugh. "Anyways, I kind of wanted to invite a guy."

Mom puts her notepad down and looks at me.

"A guy? Are you dating someone, Luna?"

"Well, not exactly, but I might be soon and..."

"And?"

"I really like him Mom," I tell her finally, and I can feel the blush creep up my face.

"Who is it? Did you finally give in and accept a date from that nice Richards boy?"

"Ew, Mom, no. Larry Richards is not nice. He's a pig and kind of a pervert."

"He is? But his family goes to church and he's been on the honor roll all through high school."

"That just proves he's a smart pervert and his family might be nice, I don't know. I just know that Larry makes my skin crawl."

"Has he done something to you, Luna?"

"Not like you're thinking, but he has made lewd comments and tried to be rough with me when I turned him down after he asked me out."

"You should have told me," Mom chastises.

"There was no point. I handled it. Actually, Gavin did."

"Gavin?"

"He's the guy I want to ask over for Thanksgiving. I really like him Mom. He's smart and funny, good looking and..."

"And?"

"He makes me laugh. *A lot.*"

"I've never heard you talk about a Gavin. Is he new at school? Maybe I can invite his mother out for brunch."

"Uh... Gavin's mom is not around. I don't think she lives in Maine anymore. He lives with his dad and brother."

"That's so sad. Maybe we can invite his entire family over?"

Panic hits me. Gavin would *hate* that. Besides that, it's going to take a lot of begging to even convince him to come to dinner alone, let alone with his brother and father—both of whom he can't stand.

"I can ask, but I think since this will be the first time you meet him, he'd rather come alone, Mom."

"You think your young man will be nervous to meet your parents?" she asks, and I smile when she talks about Gavin as 'a young man.' I doubt anyone has called Gavin that in the history of forever.

"Yeah, Mom, I think he'll be nervous."

"Then, just ask him, and we'll do our best to make him feel welcomed."

I can't help myself. I reach over and hug my mom close, grateful that she's always in my corner. I don't know what I'd do without her.

"Thank you, Mom!" I exclaim, excited that I can finally push Gavin into making our relationship public. Surely, he will see that once my parents accept him the rest will fall into place.

"If he's important to you, Luna, we want to get to know him. I'll be asking questions about him if you two start dating," Mom says and immediately guilt hits me, because we are dating—even if it's not official. Gavin is more than important to me too.

He's everything.

"Let's get through Thanksgiving. If it all goes okay and Gavin and I start dating, I'll tell you anything you want to know," I promise, suddenly feeling hopeful.

I can't wait to tell Gavin about Thanksgiving.

CHAPTER TWENTY THREE

GAVIN

"Damn, Baby, I've missed you," I growl, as we break apart. I swear every time I kiss her, I get more addicted to her. The taste of her lips haunts me continuously.

"I've missed you too," she exhales, her lips swollen from our kiss, her hair rumpled from my fingers. Her breathing is ragged, but then so is mine. These make out sessions are getting more intense. I'm trying not to push her into a direction she's not ready for, but I want her so much that I'm not sure how much longer I can hold back.

"I don't know how I'm supposed to get through the holidays without seeing you every day," I murmur, letting my thumb drift against her cheek as I hold her neck, staring at her and wishing I didn't have to let her go.

"You could come see me."

I'm lost for a minute, watching her lips move, listening to the soft sweetness in her voice. That's the only excuse I have for not understanding at first just what she's saying. When it hits me, I look at her. "Moonbeam—"

"I'm serious, Gavin. We've been seeing each other like this for a while now. You said you wanted to prove to me that you were serious, that what's between us is real."

"I did, but that's not—"

"I'm convinced, Gavin. I don't doubt you at all," she declares, her hand coming up to rest against mine on her face. "I'm completely sure in our relationship. I want everyone to know that we're together. That we..."

"What?" I ask, unable to stop myself.

"That we belong to each other."

Shit. I love the sound of that. The thought that she feels that way means more to me than I could ever tell her.

"Luna, I just don't want bullshit to pull us apart."

"As long as we're together, Gavin. Nothing can tear us apart. We just have to believe in one another."

I want to tell her that life is not that cut and dry. I want to tell her that she's being too naïve, but I can't bring myself to do that. Luna doesn't understand how hard life can be. She hasn't seen the ugly side of it, hasn't breathed it in her lungs like I do. She doesn't know, and I find that I want to protect her from that world. Only I don't know if I can.

I exhale a large breath, not wanting to disappoint her, but needing to let her down easily. If I show up at her house over the break, her parents will go through the fucking roof. Luna doesn't see it, but I'm not the kind of guy that Mr. Marshall wants sniffing around his daughter.

"I told Mom about you, Gavin."

It feels like everything inside of me stops. My heart refuses to beat, breath fails to move into my lungs.

I'm frozen.

"You told your mom?"

"I did. I mean I didn't tell her how much time we've actually been spending together, since I'm supposed to have been with Jules most of the time. But I told her that we've been talking. I told her that I really liked you and..."

"And?"

"I told her that I wanted you to come to Thanksgiving dinner."

"You told her…"

"Yep," she announces proudly.

"Luna, your mom doesn't—"

"She asked me to invite you and your dad and brother too."

"I… she what?"

"She said to invite all of you."

"I am not bringing Dad or Atticus to your parents' home, Luna."

"I know, so I told Mom that you'd be nervous enough just coming to meet them for the first time, so it would probably just be you."

"There's an understatement." I step away from her, not sure how I feel about any of this. Luna's parents are okay with me coming over? She wanted to ask my whole family? It's no secret that my dad stays drunk all of the time. Maybe that kind of town gossip doesn't get back to the Marshalls. Maybe they're too rich to hear the gossip on the common people of Stone Lake. Still, I can't believe that they're okay with me dating their daughter. Even if they don't know about my Dad, they have to know that I don't have money, that I don't have a future they would desire in a guy dating their daughter.

"Gavin?" Luna asks, nervously.

"You told her you were talking to me? You told her my name and everything? She didn't freak and demand you not be around me?"

"Gavin, I told you my parents aren't like that. You're worried over nothing. She was fine with it and Mom called and told Dad I was bringing you to dinner too. There was no freaking out, I promise."

"Luna, I don't know…"

"Please, Gavin? I want you to be at dinner. I want to spend

time with you, without having to sneak around. I want everyone to know that you're my..."

"What am I?"

"My boyfriend?" she whispers, her face flushing with embarrassment.

"Damn," I growl.

"What? You don't want to—"

"When do you want me at your house for dinner, Luna?"

"Gavin, you don't have to do this. I don't want—"

"Shh...," I whisper putting my lips to hers. "I want to have Thanksgiving dinner with my girlfriend and her parents," I tell her as I pull away. I'm kind of lying. I don't want to be anywhere near Luna's parents, but I do want to be with Luna. I love that she claims me as her boyfriend, and I love that she wants everyone to know that she's with me—that she's mine. When Luna smiles at me, it hits me that I'd walk through fire for her if it meant having her smile at me like that.

CHAPTER TWENTY FOUR

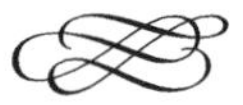

LUNA

I can hear them yelling. Mom and Dad never yell, but they're definitely yelling now. I've known for a while now that something was wrong. Mom crying at night was a clear sign that all was not right. I never in a million years thought it was this bad. The way my parents are going at it, it sounds like they hate each other. I don't understand. My entire life my parents have always been happy. They've laughed and were so much in love that my friends thought it was kind of sickening. I always envied it. I knew that when I fell in love, I wanted what they had. The kind of love that lasted, that created a family, created a world like the one I live in. I'd have kids and they'd know they had a good life and be happy. It sounds hokey, but I saw my friends live in broken homes, I saw how unhappy they were, how lost they became when one of their parents moved off. I knew I was lucky. I loved my family.

I don't know what the fight is about, they're doing their best to keep their tones hushed, but I heard Dad yelling and my mom crying and that alone makes my stomach twist in knots.

The doorbell rings and I practically run to the door.

"Hey—"

Gavin stops talking, his breath coming in a large gasp as I crash into him. He wraps his arms around me and holds me.

"What's wrong, Luna?" he asks in my ear, his voice full of worry.

"Luna, who is at the door?" Dad asks from behind me. I look up at Gavin and I know he can see the worry and stress on my face. I wish I could tell him, but I can't talk about it with Dad here.

"It's uh… my boyfriend, Dad. Gavin," I tell him, turning around. Dad's face is red, and I can see the barely controlled anger all over him. I hold Gavin's hand tightly. This is all so different. I've never seen my father so angry.

"I didn't realize we were having company for dinner," Dad says, barely sparing Gavin a glance. Gavin's hand clenches tighter in mine, and I hate that Dad is being like this. Gavin was already worried enough about meeting my family.

"I, well I asked—"

"She asked me, Arthur, and I think we're being rude to our guest," Mom says. "Hello, Gavin. It's good to finally meet you. Luna has been telling me a lot about you."

"No one mentioned anything to me about him." Dad crosses his arms over his chest and his voice still contains the anger from earlier. He's so different from the man I've always had in my life, I don't know how to react.

"You haven't been here to tell, Arthur," Mom says, and her voice may sound pleasant enough, but the look on her face is definitely filled with hurt and anger. I'm only seventeen and I can read that plain as day.

"Come on in, Gavin. It's cold out there."

"Ms. Marshall, thanks for having me," Gavin says, closing the door. He takes his coat off and I take it from him and hang it on the hall tree that Mom keeps in the foyer.

"We're glad to have you. Let's see about getting dinner on the table," Mom says. When she walks by my father, he follows her into the kitchen the yelling is low, but clearly heard.

I close my eyes and when I open them back up, Gavin is standing in front of me.

"I'm sorry," I tell him, not sure of what else to say. I'm so embarrassed and panicked over the way my parents are acting. This was not how I wanted Gavin's first dinner with us to go down.

"Babe, what's going on?"

"I swear I don't know."

"If they don't want me here—"

"*I* want you here, Gavin."

"Luna—"

"I don't know what's going on with them. Honestly, I don't. Whatever their damage is though, it's not about you, I promise."

"Babe, I'm not so sure. Your dad—"

"Trust me, Gavin. They've been fighting since Dad got back in town and you haven't been mentioned once. I don't know what is going on with them, but Dad's anger has nothing to do with you. Do you know that my parents have never fought in front of me before? *Not once...* I'm scared."

Gavin sighs then closes the distance between us, pulling me into his arms.

"I'm sorry, Babe. I truly am."

I let him hold me and put my head on his shoulder, breathing in his scent. When Gavin holds me, I feel safe and right now I need that feeling desperately.

We stay like that for a while. I'm not sure how long. We don't break apart until my father comes out of the kitchen.

"So, Gavin, tell me about yourself," he says after we all sit down in the living room. Gavin and I on the couch and Dad in a chair.

Gavin immediately tenses. I start to say something, but he beats me to it.

"Not much to tell, Mr. Marshall. I'm only nineteen. Hopefully, that will change after I graduate though."

"Nineteen? I thought Mary said you were in the same class as Luna?"

"I am."

"You were held back? Do you play sports?"

"No. Don't have much interest in them."

"So you flunked out of school?" Dad asks.

"*Dad*. Stop!"

"No. I flunked out of my Freshman year. I'm still in school and set to graduate in May. I just turned nineteen a few days ago, Mr. Marshall," Gavin answers calmly.

"A few days ago?" I gasp, feeling like the worst girlfriend in the history of girlfriends. "I didn't know. *Gavin Lodge*! How could you not tell me that it was your birthday?"

"It's just another day." He shrugs.

"It's not," I huff.

"Babe, stop," he grumbles, but he smiles at me to soften his words.

I roll my eyes and give in, but I will have to do something later to celebrate his birthday, even if it is late.

"Luna, don't you think you should go help your mom in the kitchen?" Dad asks and I frown.

"I guess so. You want to go help, Gav—"

"Gavin can stay out here with me. The kitchen is no place for men," Dad says and I pout. I want to point out that some of the biggest chefs in the world are men, but I figure the significance of that would be lost on my father. I could even point out that women hold down really powerful jobs these days, but again, I doubt he'd listen.

"I don't—"

"It's fine, Luna," Gavin says, but I can tell from the look on his face that it's really not. I lean up and kiss him gently on the lips. I know I blush deep red when I do it, because my dad is there, but I don't care. Dad's being a jerk for some reason, and I want Gavin to know that no matter what, I want him with me.

I love him… I wonder how Gavin would react if I tell him that?

Should I?

CHAPTER TWENTY FIVE

GAVIN

Well, this is going great. Luna's father doesn't like me. I'm pretty sure he might hate me. I probably shouldn't let it bother me, after all, I knew how this would go. Still, it does. Only because, Luna is special, and I plan on being a part of her life. If her father doesn't like me, that might get in the way and I don't want any obstacles between us. Atticus is a big enough one to overcome, we don't need anything else.

"What are your intentions with my daughter?" he asks and it's all I can do to keep from laughing, even if there is nothing funny about any of this. I realize I don't really date girls, but I didn't think people really talked like this. *My intentions?* Part of me wants to tell him that I intend to sleep with his daughter and take her virginity. If I told him the truth, that I intend to make her mine and take her away from Stone Lake to live the rest of my life with her, I think he'd hate that answer even more.

So instead, I shrug. "We're dating. She's an amazing girl, sir."

"She is. Luna is going places in life. I'm sure you know that. She's been on the honor roll all through school and she's already taking college AP classes."

"Yeah, I know," I tell him, not bothering to look at him, choosing to stare down at my lap instead and concentrating on my hands.

"You're Roy Lodge's boy," he says on a sneer, and he doesn't keep the disgust out of his voice.

I could tell him that I have the same disgust when it comes to my father, but I don't. I don't figure there's much use. Luna's Dad already has his mind made up about me and nothing I can tell him will change it. I don't really disagree with him. Luna is too good for me, but I'm keeping her, and I'll bust my ass to make sure that she's happy. None of that will matter to this man. I already know it. His mind is made up. If I had a daughter, I'd probably be the same.

"I am."

"Then you have to know how I feel about you hanging around my daughter."

"I figure, I know. Figure I knew before I came here today, Mr. Marshall," I tell him looking him in the eye at last.

"And yet you're still here."

"Yep. I'm still here."

"I guess we know where one another stands," he states coolly.

"I guess we do."

"Dinner is ready!" Luna calls excitedly from the other room. I walk into the dining room behind her father, wishing today was over.

"Everything okay?" Luna asks me quietly as she walks over to me and grabs my hand.

"Yeah, it's good," I lie.

"You don't look like it is," she mumbles, and I force myself to relax and smile at her.

"Quit worrying, Moonbeam."

She studies me for a minute, but slowly the tension leaves her.

"I'll make this up to you, Gavin."

I look at the beautiful girl who is holding my hand proudly, despite how her father clearly feels about me. If anyone is worth this crap, it's Luna. I lean down to kiss her cheek and I get rewarded with her blush—*and her father clearing his throat.*

It's going to be a long day…

CHAPTER TWENTY SIX

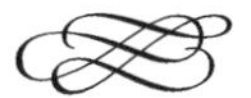

LUNA

Two Months Later

"I CAN'T BELIEVE you've been dating my brother and didn't tell me."

"Attie, we didn't want anyone to know. Not after the mess that happened when we first met."

"That's another thing. How can you date a guy that spread shit about you like that, Luna?"

"He says he didn't do it."

"And you believed him," Atticus mocks.

"I do. Gavin wouldn't lie to me. He cares about me."

"You're being naïve. Of the two of us, I know my brother better than you do, and trust me when I tell you, Luna, Gavin will always do whatever he wants, and he doesn't care who it hurts."

"That's not being fair, Attie. I know you and Gavin have issues, but he's your brother and I just think you—"

"It's because he's my brother that I know what kind of person he is. You'll regret this, Luna."

"Attie—"

"Is my brother warning you off of me again?" Gavin asks, coming up behind us, and wrapping his arms around me.

He pulls me back into him and kisses my neck. I smile despite the tenseness of the moment. His fingers slide against the chain of the locket he gave me for Christmas. It's heart shaped and inside is a picture of the two of us that Jules took one evening at her house. Jules has gone above and beyond covering for Gavin and me until we made our relationship public.

We've spent more time at her house than anywhere else, but since her parents are out of town almost every weekend, that meant Gavin and I were alone most of the time. Occasionally, the three of us would watch a movie, but that's it. Jules never invited anyone over because she knew Gavin didn't want people to know we were dating.

"I'M NOT WARNING HER, Gav, just telling her the truth," Atticus says, bringing my attention back to the present. I frown, because fighting with Attie is the last thing I want, even though Gavin warned me it would happen.

"What truth would that be?" Gavin asks, his voice sounding angry.

I hate that this is the atmosphere that Gavin lives in. I hate it for Atticus too. I wish they could see that they're both really great guys. I don't have a brother or a sister, but I've always wanted one, especially now with things so tense between my parents. I wish I could fix whatever is wrong between these two, but I have the feeling no one can.

"That you don't care about anyone but yourself."

"I think Luna knows better than that," Gavin insists, his voice low. I move my hand back and forth on his arm in silent support. "She trusts me, don't you, Luna?"

"I do," I answer without hesitation. If he needs me to tell him that, I will.

"Then, she's crazy."

"Maybe I should tell her *why* she should trust me over you, Atticus," Gavin warns, and I frown, wondering what he means.

"You might have her fooled right now, Gav, but we both know sooner or later you're going to lie to her again."

"I think you better go, Atticus," I tell him, not liking all of the animosity between them. I get enough of this kind of stress at home right now.

"Sooner or later, Luna, he's going to hurt you again."

"Attie—"

"And when he does, I won't be here to pick up the pieces again," Atticus threatens.

"I don't want you to," I tell him softly, needing to make it clear. "I've never asked you to be more than my friend, Attie. I don't think of you.... I don't care for you the way you want me to. I never have. I never will," I add softly, hoping to ease the blow. I keep my voice quiet, hating that it's all come to this, but not knowing any other way to achieve it. I need to make this clear to Atticus, so he doesn't think Gavin is what is between us. I don't want to become a war between brothers.

"Fine," he says after staring at me for a few minutes. Then, he turns and stomps off.

Jules lets out a long whistle.

"Damn, there's never a dull minute around you, is there Gavin Lodge?" she asks. Gavin doesn't answer her. I turn to face him and he's just staring in the direction his brother left.

"You okay?" I ask Gavin.

"Yeah," he says, but he sounds anything but.

"I'd say he's better than Attie. You kind of de-balled him right in front of most of our friends in the lunchroom, Luna."

"I tried to be gentle." I sigh, wishing this could have gone differently. I feel guilty.

"Trust me, he doesn't deserve your guilt, Moonbeam. Besides, if he knew he had it, he'd use it against you. That's how Atticus works."

"Gavin, your brother's not like that, at least not around us," I tell him, hating everything about this situation.

"Damn I'm suddenly glad I'm an only child," Jules responds, staring at Gavin.

"You should be," he answers in a gruff tone.

Yikes.

"I better go check on Attie. He's a bit of a whining puppy at times, but that was kind of brutal," Jules says surprising me.

"We still hanging after school tonight?" I ask her, anxious to change the subject.

"Yeah. Mom's picking us up after seventh period."

"Sounds good. Love you."

"Ditto. Later, Gavin."

"Later," he says as Jules walks away in the direction that Atticus disappeared to.

"Well, that wasn't much fun."

"It sure wasn't," Gavin agrees.

"How about we sneak into the gymnasium and make out under the bleachers?" I suggest, needing desperately to erase the dark cloud that seems to have settled over both of us.

"What about our next class?"

"I say we skip it." I grin up at him feeling brave.

"Luna Marshall, are you trying to be a bad girl?"

"You have no idea how bad," I respond. "Are you game?" I tease, backing away from him and holding out my hand.

"Lead the way," he says, threading his fingers through mine, with a grin. The smile doesn't reach his eyes, but eventually I think I can make that happen.

It'll be fun to try either way…

CHAPTER TWENTY SEVEN

JULES

"What are you doing here?" Atticus barks the minute I walk into the weight room.

Like he didn't know I'd follow him. Hell, if he wants to be honest with himself, this is why he went to the weight room to begin with. Boys are so stupid. They think with their dicks and it takes forever for their brains to finally catch up.

"I came to check on you, dickhead. Not sure why I bothered."

"I don't either, I don't want you here."

"Just because Luna shot you down in front of the whole school, doesn't mean you have to be a bastard to me, you know."

"She didn't shoot me down," he argues, and I don't even bother to hide the look on my face. He can't be that stupid and he can't expect me to be.

"Dude, she blasted you with a nuclear bomb."

"She's just confused."

"Bullshit. It's time to man up, Attie. Luna doesn't want you. She likes what your brother is giving her much more."

Perhaps I should have watched what I said a little better. I see the anger that comes over Atticus's face. It shouldn't excite me—a wiser woman would be scared, but, I like it. He reaches out and grabs me roughly. My arm will have a large bruise on it later and that thrills me too. His hand snakes out and wraps around my throat and he pushes me back against the wall hard.

"Why do you always have to be such a bitch?" he growls.

"It's a gift," I tell him, gasping to get the words out and still barely able to because his hold is so tight. I can barely breathe.

"You shouldn't tease a man, Jules. You may live to regret it."

"I don't see a man here," I mock, knowing I'm pushing him over the edge, but unable to stop myself. I want to see what he does when he loses control. At first, I thought Atticus was fun to tease. Now, I think we may be more alike than I realized.

"Such a damn bitch. Someone should have done something about your smart mouth before now." His voice rumbles and it feels like it echoes inside of me.

His lips come down hard, crushing against mine, as his tongue thrusts into my mouth. The entire time, his hand is still tight on my throat, holding me into place. I try to fight him, not because I don't want what he's doing, but because fighting him excites both of us. My fingers claw into his sides, and I know that I'm drawing blood. He bites my lip in retaliation and pain spreads through my body, making me feel alive. We kiss until we are forced to break apart, our lungs too deprived of air. He steps away from me, wiping my kiss away with the back of his hand. Attie also wipes away the smear of blood there from the wound he made on my lips.

"You're twisted," he says, staring at me, his chest heaving as he takes in oxygen.

"Takes one to know one, *lover.*" I grin at him, licking the blood from his bite.

I walk to him, my body on fire in ways it never has been before. I don't fully understand it, but I've never been the kind of girl that hides from what she wants.

"What are you doing?" he asks, his eyes narrowing as I drop to my knees in front of him.

I reach up and undo the buttons on his jeans and hold his gaze in mine, feeling powerful.

"Showing you what else I can do with my mouth," I tell him as I work the zipper down and do just that…

CHAPTER TWENTY EIGHT

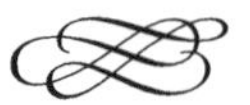

LUNA

"Jesus," Gavin huffs and I feel a little guilty.

I kiss the side of his face and hold him as his breathing slows down.

"I'm sorry," I whisper lamely. I watch as he closes his eyes. Slowly, he begins to calm and his breathing returns to normal—at least semi-normal.

"You're going to be the death of me, Luna," he mutters, but he softens his words with a brief kiss against my forehead. His arm snakes around me, his hand pressing against my arm, and he holds me to him. I can hear his heart beating rapidly against my ear.

"I know it's lame," I start, wondering how to explain things to Gavin.

"It's not lame, Luna."

"All my friends have had sex. I don't know why I keep backing out. It's not you, Gavin, you have to know that. I just..."

"Babe, stop." He moves us, so that he's leaning against the bleacher and I'm more on him now instead of the gym floor.

We're under the bleachers, having skipped class to spend some time together. Things went from innocent kissing and laughing to heavy petting and Gavin stopped things before they went too far.

Of course, he stopped them because he could feel me tensing up and withdrawing from his touch.

Because I'm a moron.

"But—"

"But nothing. You're not ready. I'm not pressuring you, Luna. It will happen when you're ready."

"You're willing to wait for me?"

"I'd wait forever if it meant you were the reward." His words touch me. Not only because they're sweet, which they truly are—but, because Gavin means them and that makes my heart swell up with emotion.

"Well, if you wait forever, then there wouldn't be any time left to claim me," I point out, trying to lighten the moment as emotion clogs my throat.

"You're such a freak," Gavin laughs.

"You like me though," I murmur looking up at him, secure in that knowledge.

"Definitely," he returns, bending down to kiss me gently on the lips.

The moment feels so perfect, so special that I can't hold back any longer.

"Gavin?"

"Luna," he says with a smile that causes his eyes to crinkle with happiness. He looks so beautiful, so heart-achingly perfect that the words come easier than I ever thought they would.

"Gavin, I think I'm falling in love with you."

The smile disappears from his face, his eyes heat with a hunger in them that makes me flush. His hand moves against the side of my neck, his fingers caressing my skin.

"I know the feeling, Moonbeam. I love you. I think I always have," he confesses.

His words wash over me, and my heart rate jumps so quickly that I think I might pass out. I don't even think, I'm not sure it's possible. Instead I move so that I slam my lips against his and I kiss him with all of the happiness surging through me right now.

Gavin loves me.

He loves me.

Nothing could be better than this.

Nothing.

CHAPTER TWENTY NINE

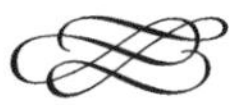

GAVIN

"I love you, too," Luna says when we finally break apart.

"Luna you don't have to—"

"It's the truth, Gavin. I love you," she vows, and I kiss her again. When I feel her hand move down between my legs, rubbing against the denim of my pants, I pull away and suck oxygen back into my lungs—and hopefully my brain.

"Babe, we have to stop. You can't miss your next class. You said you had a test," I remind her as her hand presses hard against my erection.

"I could, I mean, well… I could use my hand," she says blushing.

I pull her hand away, bring it to my lips to kiss her palm.

"Quit worrying about me. It will happen between us when it's meant to be, Luna. I'm not going anywhere. I promise you. You are more than worth the wait."

I hear the bell go off for the next class and Luna and I look at each other and frown.

"Shit," we say in unison, with a dry laugh. We're definitely going to be late.

I go first, bending down to go through the opening under the bleachers. Our gym has bleachers that fold down and there's an opening to crawl underneath them and release the levers so they will unfold. They can then slide up straight and latch against the wall of the gym. It's supposed to be state of art, I think it's kind of weird. It doesn't matter, they do have the advantage of hiding you away from others and since that private time includes Luna—I love the damn bleachers. Once I'm standing, I reach down through the opening and grab Luna's hand, to help pull her out.

"Well look what we have here," Larry Richards says from behind my back. I look around and the asshole is standing with the rest of his jock friends. There are four of them in total and there's not a one of these idiots that I like. I think they're all a waste of air.

"Shit," Luna mutters under her breath, immediately buttoning up her shirt. I had the first three buttons undone. I turn to face them, blocking her from view, but I know that they've already seen the crisp white material of her bra.

"I'd watch what you say from here out," I warn him.

I don't want to get in another fight with him, but I'm not about to walk away from another one either. They just suspended me for two days last time. Another fight will mean a longer suspension and also mean my father will have to come in. Since he's always drunk that won't go well either.

"I'm not going to say anything." He moves his shoulders up. "Don't think I need to. My boys here see the same thing I do."

"What exactly is it you think they see?"

"Whatever, man," Larry says with a slick smile that has me curling my hand into a fist. I want to knock it off of his face so much that it hurts.

"If I hear any of you fuckwads are saying one thing about Luna in this school I'll end you," I warn them.

"Gavin, let it go," Luna says quietly, putting her hand on my chest. "They aren't worth it."

"Yeah, Lodge, listen to your whore and run away."

"What did you say?" I growl, my body tense.

"Don't worry about it. We're not going to tell anyone. Hell, the whole school is already talking about it anyway."

"They are not," Luna argues.

"But they are," he says. "They can't understand why you want to keep whoring yourself out to such a loser after all of the shit he said about you. What was it, Gavin? Oh yeah, I remember now. She was dying for it. Begged you to let her suck—"

I don't let the bastard finish. I launch myself at him, slamming him against the concrete floor and connect my fist with his fucking mouth.

I'll kill him this time.

CHAPTER THIRTY

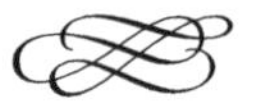

LUNA

I scream as Gavin slams on the ground, Larry under him. He grabs Larry's collar and holds him in place like that, as his fist connects with the jerk's face. Larry is pushing on him, trying to kick him—hoping to get free. Gavin doesn't give him an opening. At least until two of Larry's friends, drag Gavin off him.

I thought that was good until I see they're holding him for Larry to hit. Gavin jerks away and then, all of Larry's friends are holding him down. Larry's face is bloody and it's clear his nose is busted. I look around for something to help. There's not much, but there's an umbrella that someone must have left there during morning assembly. I grab it and before I even think about it, I take the umbrella and use it as a baseball bat, pretending his head is a baseball. I connect and it sends Larry backwards, but not enough to make him fall. He turns to look at me like he can't believe I just did that. I draw back to do it again, but Larry catches it this time and he pulls it out of my hands.

"*Leave him alone.* It's not a fair fight with you having the goon squad hold him down!" I yell. I'm so angry that I want to cry—

which is what I usually do when I get mad, and I hate that about myself.

Hate it.

"He deserves everything he's got coming to him and more," Larry says, advancing on me. Then he grabs my hair and pushes me, so I fall backwards. "Now be a good girl and stay out of it. I'll give your boyfriend back when I'm done. I doubt he'll be able to move much, but his dick will probably still work, since that seems to be all you want anyway," Larry spews as my legs connect with the bleacher and I fall. I can feel metal cut into my leg, and I cry from the pain of that more than the fall.

I hear Gavin scream, and I look up in time to see him tearing away from the guys that have him pinned. He has Larry by the arm, and he twists it. Larry screams out in pain, and I can tell from the awkward angle that it's broken. Gavin kicks him, sending him careening back into the other guys. Larry is holding his arm, screaming at Gavin about how he ruined his season, that the tournament is coming up. He's not wrong, I guess. Larry plays basketball and football. The basketball championship is coming up and the team relies heavily on his talent. I guess they'll have to find someone else.

Gavin doesn't respond with words instead he kicks Larry hard between the legs. The boys all hiss and I don't have balls but I even wince. That has got to hurt. Larry screams out, curling into a ball.

"What's going on in here?"

My face jerks up as Principal Issacs walks in the gym, his face full of anger.

Shit...

CHAPTER THIRTY ONE

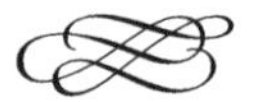

GAVIN

"Gavin, we called your father to come and get you, son."

"I figured you would," I tell the principal. My body is sore, my lip is swollen, and I'm mad at myself because I let Luna get hurt. All in all, it's been a shitty day.

"He… uh… wasn't able to come down right now. Technically, you're nineteen, but I can't let you leave school grounds alone. It's against our adopted policy. You're still a student here, despite your age."

"What you're not saying is that my father was drunk off his ass and can't drive. Hell, even if he could, he would be driving on a suspended license."

Principal Issacs looks at me while rubbing the side of his face. You can tell that the man is uncomfortable. I don't know why that brings me pleasure, but it does.

"Gavin, I know you got things stacked against you son, but you can't let that define who you are."

"Where's my daughter?" My gaze moves from Issacs to Mr. Marshall as he walks through the door.

"Mr. Marshall, I'm sorry to bother you today. I understood from your wife that you were getting ready to head out of town,"

Principal Issacs says, holding out his hand for Luna's dad to shake.

"I am. Which means I'm in a hurry. What the hell is going on in this school Issacs? Do I need to transfer Luna over into private school to make sure my daughter is protected?"

"Mr. Marshall, I can assure you that we keep a close eye on all of our student body."

"Obviously not," Luna's dad growls.

"Luna had skipped class and was in the gym at the time of the incident. There aren't supposed to be kids in the gym during that time."

"Luna doesn't skip class. She knows better," her father denies. I rub the back of my neck. Damn it, I never meant to get Luna into trouble.

"I skipped, Dad," Luna says coming out of the inner office where the principal placed her when we first got here. He kept me in the main office. Larry was evaluated by the nurse and transported to the hospital for a cast. Principal Issacs spoke with Luna quickly and after he finished talking with Larry's dad, he came in here to speak with me. I know it's bad and it's probably going to get worse. I don't really give a fuck, but I don't want the fall out to touch Luna.

"Why would you do..." he stops talking as he notices me sitting here and his face hardens as his eyes narrow and he pins me with his gaze. "You. You're at the root of this, aren't you?"

"Sir—"

"Mr. Marshall—"

"Let's go, Luna."

"Dad, I still have a class and—"

"Get your stuff and let's go, Luna, I won't tell you again."

"Mr. Marshall, Luna's not in any trouble. She'll have to attend detention the rest of the week, but—"

"I'll see that she does, but right now I'm taking her home."

"Very well, I'm sorry to delay your travel arrangements."

"You," Mr. Marshall says, ignoring Principal Issacs and instead looking directly at me. "You're no better than your father."

"Dad, *stop it*. Gavin was defending me!"

"Shut up, Luna," her father growls, and I can tell by the shocked look and the sob that escapes Luna that he's never spoken to her like that before. She goes visibly pale.

"I know exactly what you were doing with my daughter, Lodge. You're not pulling anything on me. Here's one for you, though. You stay away from my daughter. I forbid you to so much as get within a hundred feet of her."

"You won't keep me away from Luna, sir," I tell him, bitterness welling up inside and burning me.

"That's where you're wrong. If you so much as sniff the wind in Luna's direction, I'll yank her out of this school and put her in private school. You'll never see her again. Do I make myself clear?"

"Crystal."

"Gavin," Luna cries. Before I can respond to her, Mr. Marshall grabs her by the arm and hauls her out of the room.

I stare for a few minutes at the empty space where they had been standing. Then I look back at Principal Issacs.

"I'd say it's not me letting my life define who I am. I think other people do that just fine, Mr. Issacs." I tell him. "I'll call Wally's dad to come and get me."

"You'll be suspended for a week, Gavin."

"I figured."

"There may be charges filed."

"Charges?"

"You broke Larry's arm. His dad will be out for blood."

"He pushed Luna and was hurting her."

"She told me. If it comes to court, I will make them aware, but I'm just warning you what might happen. I don't think it will. I think once Mr. Reynolds hears what happened, he'll choose to lock it down."

I nod, not saying anything else.

What else could I say?

Then, I pick up the phone and call Wally's dad to ask if he could come down to the school and pick me up. I hate to do it, but when push comes to shove… I don't really have anyone else to call.

How pathetic is that?

CHAPTER THIRTY TWO

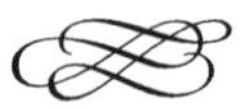

LUNA

"Is Gavin okay?" I ask Attie uncomfortably.

I don't like asking him, but I haven't spoken to Gavin since the fight at school. I know he's tried to call the house, but my parents won't let me talk to him. They took my cellphone. Gavin doesn't have a phone—cell or house, so there's no way I can call him either. My parents watch me like hawks and there's no way I can call while he's at work with them breathing down my neck. Dad's even postponed his business trip to keep me on lock-down. It's ridiculous. I don't know how to deal with them at this point.

"Are you seriously asking me that, Luna?" Attie asks, and I can tell he's pissed.

"Please, Attie."

He lets out a growling breath to show his irritation with me. I'm pretty sure he's not going to answer me, but he finally does.

"He's fine. Same old asshole. He had court yesterday."

"How did that go?"

"It didn't. The judge dropped all the charges and bitched at Richards' dad for pushing it."

"He did?" I asked shocked, but so relieved I almost feel like I can't catch my breath.

"Yeah, I guess Principal Issacs testified on Gavin's behalf. Who knows what my brother did to pull that off. Anyway, he told the judge that Gavin was only trying to pull Larry off of another student and things got out of control. When the judge found out the student was a girl..." Atticus stops talking, ending with a jerk of his shoulder.

"When does Gav get to come back to school?" Jules asks.

"Three more days." I sigh, thinking these three days are going to be the longest of my life.

"Oh, come on, Luna. It's not the end of the world."

"You aren't living with my parents. It's like I'm on prison lock-down lately."

"You could go to the movies with me and Darren Oakes tonight," Jules suggests.

"You're going out with Darren? When did this happen?"

"Eh... he's been asking me out for a while. I had my eyes on someone else, but he doesn't seem anxious to make any moves. He's all strung out over some other chick. So, I figured what the hell, I'd throw Darren a bone. At least he wants me and not some other girl."

"I'm leaving if you two are just going to talk about guys," Attie mutters, shooting me and Jules an angry look, then gets up and leaves.

"I guess I shouldn't have asked him about Gavin," I gripe.

"Oh please, if he doesn't understand by now that you are hung up on his brother and will never give him the time of day then he deserves what he gets."

"Still..."

"Luna, trust me. Attie will be fine."

"Yeah, you're right. How come you didn't tell me about Darren asking you out?"

"You've been kind of preoccupied. Besides, it's nothing. I'm not even that excited about it."

"Then, why are you going out with him?"

"I was hoping it might make the guy I like stand up and take notice. I don't think that's going to happen, though. He's too busy mooning over another chick who doesn't even know he's alive."

"Jules! You've been keeping secrets. I hate that. Who is it you like? You didn't even tell me!"

"It's silly. I don't really want to talk about it. I promise when I'm ready, I'll tell you," she says, and I frown.

We never used to keep things from each other, and I hate that we're doing it now.

"Jules—"

"Let it go, Luna. I just don't want to talk about it right now. I've never really been rejected by a guy before. Give me time to process it."

"Well he's an idiot," I protest, feeling bad.

"Yeah, most guys are," Jules jokes.

"And I don't know who the other girl is, but there's no way she's as wonderful as you," I assure her. Jules gives me a sad smile.

"Whatever. Hey, did you hear about that girl that got killed in Hagerstown?"

"Hagerstown? That's kind of close. I haven't heard anything—note my prison lockdown," I whine.

"Dude, some guy chopped her up. We're talking she had like twenty stab wounds."

"Holy crap," I mumble.

Nothing like that has ever happened this close to Stone Lake before. I can't remember something like this happening in the whole state to be honest. I mean, I don't watch a lot of the news, but still....

"Yeah, he left her naked in the snow. Police found a black rose frozen against her chest."

"Frozen? A black rose?"

"Yep, creepy stuff."

"You have to go talk to Principal Issacs," I urge her, panic hitting me.

"What are you talking about?"

"A black rose? Like the one that was in your locker? Jules you need to report it now, this is just too scary."

"Oh, come on! Getting a flower in your locker is a long way from being stabbed in the snow, Luna."

"Not that much, besides you've been getting those notes for a while too. You need to tell Principal Issacs."

"And have my parents go crazy and ruin my date with Darren? No way."

"Luna's right."

Jules and I look up to see Attie standing over us. I hadn't even heard him come back. He leans down and picks up his Algebra textbook he left lying on the cafeteria table.

"She's just being—"

"She's being smart," Atticus responds, interrupting Jules. "You need to tell him and if you won't, Luna and I will."

"Why do you care?" she asks, studying his face.

"You're my friend. I care about you," he says. Jules seems to study his face. The interaction between them is weird and it feels like there's some kind of message being transferred between the two of them that I don't get. Have I lost touch with my friends that much? I'm going to have to start doing better with that.

"It's like that," Jules says and Attie nods his head slowly.

"It's exactly like that. Either you tell or we will, Jules. This is too serious to ignore," I add, determined that she's not going to ignore the danger of this situation.

"Fine. I'll go to the office after school."

"Nope. We'll go now. All three of us."

"All of us?" Jules asks, looking at me and Attie.

"Yep all three of us. The three musketeers," I joke, smiling at the two of them.

It takes a minute, but they slowly smile too, and we all get up and dump our lunches. We walk down the hall together and I feel better. My life and my relationship with Gavin may be a mess, but I'll always have my squad.

CHAPTER THIRTY THREE

GAVIN

"I can't believe they aren't more concerned," Luna huffs, but I don't stop to see what her and Jules are talking about. Hooking my arm around her waist, I pull her against me and I turn us so that her back is pushed against the lockers and I'm pressed against her. "What—" she gasps, but I don't let her finish. Her mouth is open, and I want in there, so I claim her lips, thrusting my tongue into her sweet depths and kiss her with all the pent-up hunger I have.

Which is a lot.

I haven't seen her in eight days.

Eight fucking days.

I haven't spoken to her. I haven't seen her. I haven't had any contact at all with her.

I got desperate a few times and wanted to ask Atticus about her, but I knew it wouldn't do any good. Having her in my arms again feels like heaven.

"Gag," Jules mutters. I want to ignore her, but Luna pushes against me and I step back, releasing her mouth, but keeping her in my arms.

"You're back," Luna whispers. "I missed you so much."

"God, I missed you too, Moonbeam," I tell her, not even bothering to try and play it cool.

"Damn the great Gavin Lodge is pussy whipped," Jules mumbles and we turn around to look at her.

I scowl, because I don't like that term, especially in reference to Luna. She deserves better.

"Shut up, Jules," Luna laughs, turning, but staying in the circle of my arms. "What are you going to do about your parents?"

"There's nothing to do. I told you and Attie before, this was a waste of time."

"It's not. *It's serious*. I can't believe your parents are being such morons."

"What's going on?" I ask, completely lost.

"Jules has gotten two notes in the last three days from her stalker."

"Did they threaten her?"

"No, but..."

"But what?"

"They had the black roses, just like that girl in Hagerstown."

"What happened in Hagerstown?"

"Don't you ever watch the news, dude?"

"Not really." I shrug. I'm not about to explain we're lucky to keep the electricity on most months, forget about television.

"There was a girl murdered in Hagerstown. She was stabbed repeatedly like twenty times and for some reason Attie and Luna think the same thing will happen to me."

"I uh..." I don't know exactly what to say to that, I'm kind of siding with Jules. That seems like a huge jump in thought.

"Don't you get it," Luna says. "That girl—who was stabbed twenty-four times by the way—was found naked in the snow with a black rose on her chest."

"Oh... Had she been getting notes like Jules?" I ask, kissing the top of Luna's forehead... because I can.

It really feels fucking great to have her in my arms again. I felt like I was dying without her.

"No," Jules says. "Which is exactly why my parents aren't worried and why Luna needs to knock it off. She's starting to freak me out," she adds, slamming the door to her locker.

"I'm sorry. I just can't believe your parents are leaving you this weekend."

"They go out of town every weekend, you know that, Luna."

"I know, but after you told them about the notes and the rose...."

"Maybe we could come stay with you this weekend," I suggest. I'm not sure Luna has a right to be this worried, but I have to admit, it is kind of freaky.

"You just want an excuse to come shag at my house," Jules says rolling her eyes.

"He does not, but it wouldn't work anyway," Luna sighs out.

"Why not?" I ask, frowning.

"I'm on house lockdown until further notice."

"Shit."

"Yeah, until Dad can determine that we are no longer seeing each other, I'm not allowed to leave the house. I went out to get the mail from the mailbox yesterday and I thought he was going to stroke out about it."

"We're not breaking up, Luna."

She looks up at me, sadness on her face, her hand moving to rest against the side of my neck.

"I know. They'll give this up eventually. They'll have to."

"What if they don't?"

"I'll be eighteen soon and it won't matter."

"You won't be eighteen until May, Luna. That's like three months away—almost four. I missed your last birthday because we weren't talking. I'm not going to miss this one—parents or no parents," I warn her.

"You won't miss it."

"How do you know?"

"My birthday falls right before prom this year," she says with a grin. "And I'm not missing my senior prom. I'm going with my boyfriend. My parents aren't going to ruin it for me."

"Luna—"

"And neither are you," she mumbles, giving me a fake scowl.

"You're really going to make me go to that shit?"

"Yep, tux and all. So, you better start saving up that money you're making from the extra hours your boss has been giving you."

"Christ."

"Pussy whipped," Jules singsongs.

"Sounds like it," Atticus says dryly, and I tense as he joins us. "Down big brother, things are cool," he says taking in my face. My eyebrow goes up in disbelief and he shrugs. "Luna's made it clear we're just friends, and I'm good with that. I'm seeing someone else now and I like her."

"Who are you seeing?" Jules asks him, her eyes narrowing.

"None of your business," Atticus laughs and for some reason he seems to be taking a lot of pleasure in his announcement. The asshole probably isn't even seeing anyone and is trying to get Luna's attention.

"That's so great, Attie. I hope you've found someone that treats you like you deserve."

God, there's so much I could say to that.

"I'm happy," Atticus affirms, and something seems different about him. He's almost calm. Hell, maybe he has found someone. I don't care, but if it makes living with him easier, I'm all for it.

"Great, everyone is happy," Jules mumbles. "I'm out of here."

"Jules—"

"Give it a rest, Luna. I'm fine. I'm going out with Darren again tonight. He'll keep me safe from any knife wielding psychos."

Jules takes off after that and Atticus lifts his shoulders to show his indifference.

"I guess I'm out of here too. Later, Luna. Gavin… let's hope I don't see you again today."

"Finally, something we agree on," I mumble and the bastard laughs. Something has definitely changed.

"Bye, Attie!" Luna calls.

"Well, that was different."

"Atticus will get better, wait and see. He just needed time to get used to you and me as a couple."

I don't point out that my issues with my brother started long before I spoke one word to her. I don't want to waste more time talking about him. It's not important. There are other things on my mind.

"Are we a couple?"

"Of course we are. Why would you ask that? Do you want to break up with me, Gavin?"

I study Luna's face and I see the distress there. I sigh.

I kiss her lips quickly, just a touch, not giving in and tasting her again—as much as I want to.

"No. But you said your parents…"

"So, we'll work around them. I'm not giving you up, Gavin."

"We can't hide our relationship forever, Luna."

"They'll accept us eventually, Gavin."

"And if they don't?"

"Then, it won't matter. I'll have graduated high school and we'll start our lives together."

"You'd be willing to leave Stone Lake with me?" I ask her, my voice intense and hope causing my heart to beat faster.

She looks at me and for a minute I see something flash in her eyes. I don't know how to read it, but it's gone as quickly as it appeared.

"I'd be willing to go anywhere with you, Gavin. I love you."

It feels like I'm breathing easy for the first time in my life. I kiss her then, pouring everything she makes me feel into the action.

Jules can call it pussy whipped, I don't care.

The truth is, I don't want to spend one day without Luna in my life.

CHAPTER THIRTY FOUR

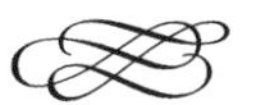

LUNA

"How long do we have?" Gavin asks, and I immediately feel guilty.

We've been keeping our relationship a secret for the last month and a half. After that first day at school, we've taken great pains to not be seen together there. I didn't know it at the time, but when I got home that evening my parents gave me hell about making out with Gavin in the hallway. I don't know if it's one of the teachers or students that have made it their mission to make sure my parents know what I'm doing, but Gavin and I spend our days barely acknowledging each other and stealing time away whenever possible.

Tonight, I'm at Jules' house.

My father had to go back out of town and my mother relented, letting me spend the night with Jules on the condition we didn't leave her house. Technically, I've not. Gavin brought us take out and we ate in Jules room. Jules is out with Darren, so we've enjoyed the place to ourselves.

I look at the clock beside the bed and frown.

"Jules will probably be back in an hour or so," I tell him.

"Hey, don't sound so sad. An hour is an hour. This is the best night I can remember having in forever."

"I know. I just hate that we have to hide being together."

"Yeah," he says, lifting my hand off his chest and holding it so it is flat against his. Then, he stretches his hand flat against mine, palm against palm, fingers against fingers, before slowly threading them together, bringing my hand to his lips. "Someday soon, we'll leave Stone Lake behind, Luna. We'll start over just you and me."

"You sound so sure of yourself."

"I am. Together, there's nothing we can't conquer. We'll have each other, that's all we will need."

"Where will we live?"

"Anywhere we want. Somewhere warm and sunny."

"I do like the sound of that. And by the water."

"Yeah, definitely close to the water," he says his blue eyes crinkling at the corners.

"Are you going to school?"

"I've been thinking about that," he murmurs.

"And?"

"I think I want to be a cop, Luna."

"A cop?" I ask, surprised.

"Yeah. When I had my court hearing? I got to sit back and watch a few cases and watched these detectives testify. It was interesting and it felt like..."

"Like what?"

"Like they were making a difference. I'd like that. I'd like to know what I was doing was making a difference. That sounds stupid I guess."

"I don't think it sounds stupid at all."

"You don't?"

"Nope. I don't at all. I think you'd make a great detective."

"Well, I don't know if I'd ever get the training and experience to be a detective, but—"

"Bull hockey. You could be a detective or even an FBI agent like on television."

"FBI?" he laughs.

"Definitely. You can do anything you want to do, Gavin Lodge."

"You have that much faith in me?"

I roll so I'm lying on top of him and we're gazing at each other. I let my fingers sift through his dark wavy hair.

"I have complete faith in you, Gavin. I think you would rock being an agent." I grin down at him, biting on my lip, then change my voice as if I was an announcer. "FBI Agent Gavin Lodge."

I think I see him blush a little, and he shakes his head a little looking up at the ceiling.

"You're crazy."

"I can see it now. I'll go out to the grocery store and all the women will be whispering."

"They will, huh?"

"Oh, that's the wife of FBI Agent Gavin Lodge. He just brought down an entire terrorist cell all by himself."

"I'm not sure I'd want to deal with terrorist cells," he laughs.

"Well, whatever," I mock.

"I do like one part of that sentence though."

"What was that?" I whisper, loving how his eyes go darker and his voice gets a gravely texture to it when he talks lows. It sends chills of awareness over my body. My gaze immediately zeros in on his lips, and I watch them move as he talks. He really is the most beautiful man I've ever seen in my life.

"The wife part."

"Oh… I uh… I didn't mean that you had to—"

"I like it, Luna."

"You do?" I ask, having trouble breathing.

"Fuck yeah, I do."

"Okay then." I grin, smiling so big that it's almost painful.

"It may be bumpy to begin with, Luna. But you need to know

that I don't care if we have to live in my truck at first, whatever I need to do, I will do to give you the world."

"Live in your truck?" I ask, wondering how that would work. Not that I mind, if that was what we would have to do to be together, then we'd do it.

"Starting out maybe. I'd make sure you were safe, though. I'd get a job, two or three if I needed to. I'm not afraid of hard work, Luna. Even if it was sweeping floors and washing dishes, I will find a way to get money together so we could rent a nice place. I'd take care of you, I swear."

"I can get a job too. I want to help, Gavin. It will be our future."

"Ours," he agrees.

"I love you," I murmur as his lips come down on mine. He doesn't give me the words back, but he shows me that he feels the same by the way he kisses me and that's more than enough.

CHAPTER THIRTY FIVE

GAVIN

"Where have you been?"

Atticus looks up at my question as he closes the window. I had the glass cut for it and repaired it a couple months back. I think I did a pretty good job, considering I'd never tried anything like that before. I look at the clock on my table and it's almost four in the morning. I didn't get back from Jules until around two. I didn't want to leave Luna. Jules came home, however, and I headed out. I didn't expect to find my brother wasn't home yet. It's not that I care really, but it's peculiar for him to be out this long. He's up to something, he's been way too laid back lately—especially about me and Luna.

"My how the tables have turned. I guess this is the part where I tell you that it's none of your business."

"Whatever," I respond with a shrug. He wants to be secretive, I don't give a damn. I'm actually just thankful he's given up causing problems between me and Luna.

"Does Dad know that I've been gone?"

"You mean, did I rat you out?"

"Yeah," Atticus presses, kicking off his shoes and throwing his coat on the floor.

"Nah, he's been passed out most of the night," I tell him. "He was still sleeping it off when I got home."

"Nothing like being able to rely on dear old Dad."

"Yeah. Can you remember Atticus?"

"Remember?"

"Was he ever different? When Mom was here, I mean? Or was he always..."

"A drunken lush?" Atticus supplies and I nod in agreement.

There's silence for a while as Atticus gets in bed. I figure he's not going to answer. I kind of regret that because this is the first decent conversation we've had in forever. It's almost... *nice.* He doesn't have the stored-up anger he always spews at me.

"Gavin?"

"Yeah?"

"You won't keep Luna."

"Let it go, Atticus," I grumble. I should have known better. Atticus will never change.

"I'm not saying it to be a bastard. Well, maybe I am a little. I really care about Luna, but I'm just saying, whatever plan you're cooking up in your head. It won't happen."

"Why is that?"

"Because Luna loves her parents. She'll never go against them and her Dad will never accept you for his daughter. Never."

"You're wrong. Luna will always choose me. We're going to go away together."

"She may talk about it, but she'll never leave Stone Lake. This is her home and..."

"Just say it and get it over with, Atticus."

"If you convince her to leave, she'll end up hating you for it. Luna's not like us. She doesn't know how hard life is. If she goes away with you, that's all she'll ever have. You'd do better to let her go now."

I don't respond. In my heart, I'm arguing he's wrong. He doesn't understand. The love that Luna and I share is special. It's strong enough to survive whatever life throws at us. I'll work hard to make sure nothing touches her. It won't be easy, but nothing worthwhile is.

In my head, however, there's this little voice that nags Atticus is right.

Fuck.

CHAPTER THIRTY SIX

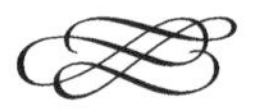

LUNA

"Crap, Gavin, duck!" I urge him as quietly as I can, pulling on his arm, and we dive behind his truck.

"What in the hell?" Gavin asks, looking at me like I'm completely crazy.

"Dad's walking into the school," I hiss, peeking over the rim of his truck bed.

Gavin releases an angry breath and then, he stands up. I panic immediately and jerk so far down that my butt hits the ground.

"What are you doing? *Get back down here,*" I order him in an angry whisper.

"I'm not hiding on the ground like an idiot, Luna."

"He'll see you!"

"Maybe. He won't see you though, unless you want to just stand up and face him like I'm willing to do."

"Gavin, stop. Why are you talking like this? You know what will happen if Dad finds out we're still seeing each other."

"Do I, Luna? We don't really know do we?"

"What is wrong with you?"

"I'm tired of hiding the fact that you and I are dating. I'm tired of being your dirty little secret," he growls, looking down at me with anger, and I feel the hurt I've caused him. Guilt washes over me.

"I'm going to tell them, Gavin, I swear."

"When? We've been sneaking around like this—"

"It's not been that long, Gavin," I defend.

"It's been almost three months, Luna. Three months I've been this dirty little secret, only seeing you on the weekends when you go over to your girl's house," he growls.

I wish I could say this is coming out of left field, but I know that it's not. Gavin has been getting increasingly upset over keeping our relationship under wraps. He hates that I talk to Jules and Atticus through the day but have to walk past him like I don't even see him. I hate it too, it tears me up to ignore him, but I think he doesn't see that part of it.

"I'm going to tell them, Gavin, I swear. I love you."

"Do you? I don't see you going up to your father and telling him about us. I don't see you doing anything to change any of this. All I see is you hiding."

"You're not being fair, Gavin."

"I don't feel like being fair. I'm nineteen. I am not some scared kid that's going to crawl on the ground to hide the woman who *says* she loves him."

"If I tell my father we're still seeing each other, he'll transfer me to private school, and I'll never get out of the house. Then, we'll never see each other. Is that what you want, Gavin?"

"You should get up, Luna. You better go see what your Dad is here for," he says, turning away from me and getting inside his truck.

That panic inside of me gets worse and three words reverberate in my brain.

This is bad.

Why does it feel like I'm losing Gavin? I don't know how to fix this. I don't know what to do. All I know is that if I walk away from here, I might lose him forever.

That thought is terrifying…

CHAPTER THIRTY SEVEN

GAVIN

Damn it.

I know I'm not being fair. I know I'm being an asshole. Luna doesn't deserve this, not really. But, Christ! What man wants to cower down beside his truck and hide like a damn kid. I'm not a kid anymore and despite what Luna's parents think, I could be good for Luna. I could…

In my head, I hear Atticus's voice from months ago telling me that Luna will never choose me—that she will always pick her parents and Stone Lake. I've heard them over and over constantly ever since he first said them, and I can't seem to shake them. I love Luna. I live for every moment I get with her, and as the months pass and we get closer to her birthday, to prom and ultimately graduation the time for her to decide is closer. Does she already know her decision? She says she'll go with me. She says she doesn't even need to think about it, but is she telling the truth? Is the future of us as real to her as it is to me? I can't be sure, and to be honest, I'm not confident she will choose me. I'm actually starting to believe Atticus is right. Luna will pick her parents and staying in Stone Lake. I wake up in the middle of the night from nightmares of Luna saying goodbye to me.

"Gavin, stop," Luna says, standing up and standing at my truck door.

Her voice is muffled, and I should just leave, but I've already been a big enough dick. I crank the window down and stare at the girl I love more than breathing. She has no idea how bleak my life is here. She doesn't know that Atticus and I weren't able to keep the electricity on this last month and we've been sleeping under blankets and all the clothes we can fit on our bodies at one time. Last night I had on three pair of pants and thermal underwear. I've been at school all day and yet, my balls are still fucking frozen. I tore Atticus away from my father last night. Atticus came in late and Dad caught him and started beating the shit out of him. My brother might have been able to hold his own, but Dad caught him by surprise by hitting him across the back with a baseball bat. If he had gone higher and hit his head, chances are that Atticus wouldn't be here. I've got bruises under my clothes from Dad's licks, getting even with me for interrupting the fight, but I put the old man on his ass and got Atticus out of there.

I didn't talk to my brother, I didn't say another word to my father. There was really nothing to say. This is our life. This is what we have, and I can't keep staying here. I have to get away. The only thing here for me is Luna...

And if she doesn't choose me... I don't know what I'll do.

"Gavin..." she says again, when I don't reply.

"It's okay, Luna," I tell her, feeling so empty inside that I'm not sure I have the energy to keep carrying on this conversation. "I'll see you tomorrow." I start up my truck, needing to escape.

"It's not okay. You're upset."

I take a deep breath.

"You're going to have to tell them soon, Luna. It won't be long until we graduate."

"I will tell them, I promise. I just... I can't do it right now, Gavin. I can't. We have to wait."

"What will waiting change?"

"Well for one, I'll be eighteen. They can't truly tell me who I can see and who I can't when that happens."

"There's not that big a difference between eighteen and seventeen, Luna."

"Gavin, I promise. Just give me until my birthday please? That's not that far away."

"Be honest with me, Luna. Are you really planning on leaving Stone Lake with me?" She swallows, I can see the movement of her throat. I see the bleakness in her eyes, and it feels like I've been sucker punched. "You're not planning on leaving at all, are you, Luna? It's all just been some make-believe fantasy in your head," I mutter, shifting my truck into gear.

"It's not! You don't know what might happen. Maybe once we tell my father that we're together and that's not changing. He might accept you. He might accept us. There's a chance, you know."

"There's zero chance in that happening, Moonbeam."

"It could, Gavin," she pleads desperately, and I close my eyes against the grief I see on her face. Atticus is right, I'm already causing her heartache and I never wanted to do that.

"Luna, let's pretend for a moment that he does. He's okay with us dating, okay with us moving in together, all of it. I still have to leave Stone Lake. I have to get away from my father, from Atticus. I'll still be leaving."

"Gavin—"

"I'm asking if you will, Luna? Will you be leaving? Will you leave with me and live the life we've talked about?"

"I told you I would," she murmurs.

"You have. I'm just not sure I believe it."

"If leaving Stone Lake is the only way to be with you," she whispers.

"Yeah?"

"I will leave and not look back. I'd choose you over everything, Gavin. I promise you, I'd always choose you over all of them." I let her words wash over me. In the back of my mind there's still that doubt, but I do my best to push it aside. "I love you," she adds, leaning in so her head rests against mine, her fingers brushing against my skin.

"I love you too, Luna," I promise, whispering in her ear, then I kiss her lips lightly.

"Go into the school and see what your Dad wants. We'll talk tomorrow."

"We're okay?" she asks.

"We're okay," I assure her, praying that it's true.

She gives me another brief kiss and with a sad smile, I pull away.

When I look in my rearview mirror, I see Luna standing there. She watches me for a minute then enters the school.

Going to her father... As I'm driving away.

I hope that's not how it's always doomed to be...

CHAPTER THIRTY EIGHT

LUNA

"Dad? What are you doing here?" I ask him, breathless because I ran up the stairs to the school entrance.

I'm fighting tears, too. I'm sure that doesn't help. Gavin might have said we were okay, but I saw the bleakness on his face. I put that look there. I know he can tell that I don't really want to leave Stone Lake. At the same time, I can't stop myself from hoping that I'm worrying over nothing. I have this fantasy in my head, that something happens and magically my parents will love Gavin as much as I do, and my Dad will offer him a job or help him to get training to be a cop here in Stone Lake and it will all work out. I can keep Gavin and stay in the place I love.

After the conversation I had with Gavin, that seems even more impossible now…

"I came to pick my girl up and drive her home."

"Oh, I was planning on hitching a ride with Jules…"

"I have something I want to talk over with you, Luna."

All of the sudden, a chill moves over me. Can they know about me and Gavin? Dad's face has a look on it that I've never seen before. Even when he and Mom are fighting there's a softness on his face when he talks to me. That's definitely not there right now. Right now, he seems remote and sad.

He seems really sad.

"Uh... just let me get my things from my locker," I whisper.

I leave him standing there and go to my locker to grab what I need to take home for the weekend. I was hoping I'd be able to spend tomorrow at Jules since it's Saturday. The look on Dad's face makes me wonder if that's going to be an option.

"You ready to roll?" Jules asks, coming up behind me laughing as I slam my locker shut.

"I uh... Dad's here to pick me up, Jules."

"Crap."

"Yeah," I whisper.

"Do you think he knows that you and Gavin are seeing each other?"

"No... I mean I don't think so? I don't see how he could. I guess it's possible, but—"

"Luna, you're babbling."

I stick my tongue out at her and give her a worried smile. "Honestly, it feels like something is wrong Jules. I'm kind of worried."

"Okay, go talk to him. You will call or text me the minute you know what's up, right?"

"Yeah..."

"You have minutes left to text me, right?"

"Yeah."

"Good. Give me a heads up, ASAP, girl. And don't worry, it's going to be fine."

"Even you don't sound like you believe that," I tell her, walking back towards the front office with her.

"Okay, I admit your dad showing up isn't the greatest of signs. He's usually away on business all the time."

"That's what I'm worried about," I confide, keeping my voice down, shoving my books against my chest and holding onto them like they're a lifeline. I hold my chin against them, biting on my bottom lip in worry.

"Still, it doesn't necessarily mean anything bad. Don't worry about anything, until you have something to worry about. Right?"

"Right."

We walk the rest of the way in silence and when we get to the office Jules gives me a quick hug.

"Hey, Mr. Marshall, you're looking good!" Jules calls out, a little too peppy.

"Hey, Julie. Drive safe going home," he says, his voice solemn. I turn to Jules with my eyes wide and see the same mini-freak-out on her face.

"Call you later, Jules."

"Sure thing, chicken wing," she says with a grin and heads outside.

"Are you ready, Luna?"

"Ready as I'll ever be, Dad," I tell him and pray I'm telling the truth.

CHAPTER THIRTY NINE

ATTICUS

"You free tonight?"

"Who's asking?" Jules quips as I stop her from getting into her car.

"Not in the mood for your bullshit tonight, Jules," I warn her.

"Gee, Attie, maybe I'm not in the mood for yours."

"What's that mean?"

"It means, I haven't heard from you in weeks. I'm not just some whore you can call when you want to screw."

"That's exactly what you are. Don't forget you started this," I warn her.

"Then, I'm finishing it."

"Bullshit."

"I mean it. I've been dating Darren for a while. He's a good guy and he likes me. He sure as hell doesn't treat me like a whore."

"I treat you exactly the way you like, and we both know it."

"Well, maybe I want more now."

"Then I'll give you more tonight," I respond, grabbing her arm and pulling her into my body roughly, my hand sliding under the short skirt she's wearing. My finger pushes against the thin lace strap of her thong as I massage her ass.

She shoves me away and my eyes narrow on her.

"What is your damage? I told you I've been dating Darren. We can't let him find us together."

"What's it matter? It's me you want. You can't tell me that straight-laced football player knows how kinky you like it, Jules."

"Yeah, but sex isn't everything. We're getting ready to graduate. Darren has a promising career as a quarterback. He's had pro scouts come check him out already."

"You've got to be fucking kidding me."

"What? I can't want better for myself?"

"I'm out of here," I growl, sick of the fucking bitch. She was only good for a quick release anyway. I'll find a different one. I don't need her shit.

"Don't be like that, Attie. We can still have fun, just not as often."

"Forget it. I got bitches lined up. You're easily replaced, Jules. Whores always are," I tell her over my shoulder, not bothering to turn around. She's not worth my time.

I head out walking. I don't live far from the school. It's actually less than a mile until you turn off the road. It's only once you do take that turn it's another three miles to get to the house. Our house is the very last one too, which works great for my dad because people don't see him drinking until he passes out or hear him screaming at all hours of the night. Probably the thing he likes the most is that he can beat the shit out of us without anyone calling the cops.

I'm still fucking sore from the baseball bat he used on me last night. I was stupid. The son of a bitch hasn't gotten the drop on me like that in a while. I wasn't expecting him to hit me from behind. I went down so hard, and I couldn't seem to recover, not until he was already whaling into me.

The beatings used to be pretty regular, but since Gavin and I got older I think the asshole is afraid of us. If I'm honest he's probably more afraid of Gavin. He's never really respected me and someday I'll make him pay for that.

I make it to the edge of our driveway right as I see Gavin get out of his old junk heap of a truck. He seems preoccupied and he's definitely not paying attention to what's around him. You would think that our lives would teach him better than that. He and Luna must be fighting. That thought fills me with joy that I can't even begin to express, and I find my lips moving into a smile. I don't bother to try and hide it. No one is watching me anyway. I move and hide behind the large Ash tree I'm standing beside. I don't want my father to see me. I see him standing there behind the run-down old storage shed at the edge of our yard. He's standing there holding a shovel and he's watching every move that Gavin makes. In just a few steps, Gavin will be right in front of him. Gavin has no idea.

I guess after the way Gavin stepped in to help me last night, I should probably warn him, but I don't. I stand there and watch as Dad swings the shovel back and slams it into the back of Gavin's head. To prove I'm an even bigger bastard than maybe I knew, my smile deepens as Gavin falls to the cold ground like dead weight. Maybe it did kill him, it certainly connected with him hard enough. A world without my brother in it. It'd tear Luna all up. She'd need a shoulder to grieve on. She'd need someone who had suffered the same loss. We could bond… eventually she'd see that it was me that she should have been with all along… Suddenly, I wish it was me that swung the shovel and connected with my brother's skull.

The shovel clangs against the rock pavers and my dad starts kicking Gavin repeatedly with his work boots.

"Thought you could jump in and stop your brother from being punished. Now you'll take his punishment and your own. You're not the ruler here. You aren't nothing but a waste of fucking space. Can't even help your old man keep a roof over our heads. You're a fucking rock around my neck holding me down."

He keeps yelling, his words sometimes slurring and other times crystal clear. I could help Gavin. Instead I back away, making sure to stay hidden behind the tree and when I am out of eyesight, so that there's no way my father can see me and change his target, I take off running.

With any luck maybe he'll kill Gavin and die of a heart attack himself.

CHAPTER FORTY

LUNA

It feels like somebody has died. Looking up at the somber faces of my parents, seeing the tears in my mother's eyes, that's the only explanation I can come up with. Immediately I think of my grandmother. Her health hasn't been great since she fell. This was the first holiday we've missed with them in forever.

"Is it Gramma?" I ask, fear in my voice. In my mind, I can see her sweet face, her dark hair varying shades of gray now, her eyes soft behind her glasses and her favorite pink flowered apron tied around her. She was always so soft. I'm not sure how a person can be as soft as she is, but when you hug her it felt like you were surrounded by feather pillows.

"What? No, Moonbeam, Gramma's fine. We'll be seeing her soon."

"Then, what's going on?" I ask even more confused.

"I... Well... You see..." Mom's stuttering and all my attention is on her and maybe it's because of that I wasn't prepared for my dad, or maybe just hearing the words is what hurt me and there's no way to get prepared for them...

"Your mother and I are getting a divorce," he says, and it feels like the world begins crumbling around me.

"But... you two love each other. We're happy," I insist, even knowing that they've not been happy for months and months.

Every night that my mother has been crying in her room at night, comes back to haunt me. The constant sadness on her face, the way my father has been gone constantly. It all begins to add up. I mean, I knew something wasn't right, but I never in a million years thought my parents would get divorced.

"We still love each other," my dad says.

My mother snorts out a bitter sound that hurts to hear. When I look at her, the sadness is still in her eyes, but on the rest of her face it has been replaced with anger.

Cold anger.

"Don't lie to our daughter, Arthur. Not like you've been lying to me all these months," she accuses.

"Lyndie—"

"Lydia," my mother corrects him, her voice harsh.

My mother's name is Lydia, but for as long as I've been on this earth, Dad has always called her Lyndie. For a second, he looks like Mom has slapped him by taking that away. I suck in a deep breath, because it feels like *I'm* the one who was slapped.

"I do love my daughter," Dad says, roughly.

"Oh, that's right. You love your daughter, it's just your wife you left for your whore."

That's when the truth hits me. That's when I know that my father is truly leaving. We won't be a family anymore, because he has another woman. Everything I've ever known is suddenly changing. My life is falling apart.

"Lydia, stop! What's between us, doesn't involve our child."

"But it does," I yell, standing up, tears in my eyes. "You're destroying my life."

"Luna—"

"Moonbeam—"

"I *hate* you," I scream. "I *hate* you both!"

It feels like the words are being torn from me. I can't see them, there are too many tears in my eyes. I run from the house, slamming the front door and I take off sprinting. I've never been there, but I'm going to Gavin's. I need him.

He's all I have...

CHAPTER FORTY ONE

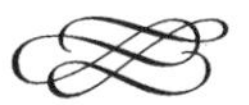

LUNA

I ran almost all the way to Gavin's, but no one was home. I started to go to Jules' house, but I remembered that she had a date with Darren. So, I kept walking and somehow, I ended up at the old dock in front of Stone Lake.

The place where I was first held by Gavin.

I'm feeling more than a little lost. I'm so cold, I don't think I'll ever be warm again, but I can't go home. Not now... I don't want to see my parents. There are things I'll need to talk to them about... but not right now.

"Get out of here."

"Gavin?" I gasp jumping. I search the area. Then I find him, standing in the shadows, looking over the water—his back to me.

"What are you doing here, Luna?" he asks, still not turning around. He's standing at an awkward angle. His hand is folded against this stomach. He seems off and his voice is different.

"I had a fight with my parents."

"Must be the night for it," he says and he laughs. His laugh immediately turns into a cough, he wheezes next. "Fuck," he mutters.

"Gavin, what's wrong?"

"Got into a fight with my old man," he says and that's when he turns around to face me.

I cry out before I can stop myself. It's not dark yet. There's enough shadows around the copse of trees he's standing near to somewhat hide him, but there's definitely enough light to see that Gavin has been beat up. His lip is busted, his right eye is swollen, there's a cut under his chin, and the blood has pooled and dried. There are varying degrees of bruising on his face and neck that disappear in a trail under his shirt. He's holding his hand at an awkward angle, and I don't even know how he's still standing.

"Where's your truck, Gavin?"

"I parked it in the clearing beyond these trees," he says, his voice sounding lifeless as he looks over the water.

"You need to go to the hospital," I tell him. "Let's go and I'll drive you."

"I'm not going to the hospital."

"You need someone to look at your injuries."

"I've had enough of adults, Moonbeam."

"Your dad's not an adult. He's scum," I growl.

"Yeah, on that we can agree."

"Give me your keys. I'll take us to Jules'—"

"I don't want anyone to see me like this, Luna. Not tonight at least. Besides," he adds giving me a sad attempt of a smile. "I don't think my body could take you driving my stick shift."

I know he's trying to be funny, but seeing him standing in front of me in so much pain, I'm not finding anything amusing about it at all.

"Hand me your keys, Baby," I murmur to him. "I'll go get a blanket."

"Luna—"

"I'm cold, Gavin."

He uses his good hand—at least it's in better shape than the other one—and reaches in his pocket to get his keys. He hands them to me, and I go up on my tip toes to kiss his cheek.

"You've never called me baby before," he says. "I like it."

"I love you, Gavin," I whisper, needing him to know that. "I'll be right back."

I run to his truck and find two old blankets and a pillow that we keep thrown in the back. When you have to hide to see one another, you get pretty creative and pillows and blankets become a must. Once I have them, I head back to the dock. I take the thickest blanket—which really isn't great, they're both pretty ratty—and spread it out on the dock and then place the pillow down on it.

"Let's get you lying down," I tell him, and he looks at me.

"Moonbeam, I'm not sure I can and if I do get down, I'm not positive I can get up."

Anguish fills me. I think I could kill Gavin's father right now. I know realistically I wouldn't be able to, but I think I could at least make it hurt.

"You should have called me, Gavin. I would have come to you."

"You were with your father. That would have been rich, right? The secret boyfriend calling for help because his drunk father waylaid him with a shovel."

"He did this with a shovel?" I growl.

"I wasn't conscious through most of it, but when I woke up there was a shovel on the ground beside me, so..." he shrugs. "Luna, just let it go. Your parents will be wondering where you are and—"

"My parents can go to hell," I mutter as I help take his weight and we hobble over to the blanket.

It takes some work, but we finally get him sitting. He cried out in pain a couple of times and each noise broke my heart. There are tears falling down my cheeks and my hands are shaking, but I'm doing the best I can to hold myself together. I help him out of his tennis shoes and carefully remove his jacket, followed by his shirt.

When I see the dark colored skin that has already set in bruising, I lose it. I know that it will only get worse and tears run down my face unchecked.

"I hate him," I murmur, kissing the worst spots as lightly as I can.

"Join the crowd," Gavin hisses as I kiss the largest bruise which is on his chest and moves along his collar bone.

"I need a first aid kit."

"I don't think that will help, Luna," Gavin says with a dry laugh that immediately causes him more pain.

"Do you think anything is broken?"

"Maybe a rib, but no. My hand is sprained pretty bad, but I'll be okay."

"We need to—"

"I'll be okay, Moonbeam. This isn't the first time, it's just the first time in a while."

"What do you mean?"

"I let my guard down. I was distracted. If I'd been watching, he never would have got me."

"You were distracted because of me."

"Luna, it doesn't matter. I was just—"

"Thinking about our fight," I finish for him.

Gavin's good hand comes up and he moves a finger across my lip.

"Let it go, Luna. My father is a bastard. This is not your fault and I don't want you blaming yourself. Dry up your tears, please," he adds, wiping a couple away. "He doesn't deserve them."

"I love you, Gavin."

"I love you. I always will," he says, and I can feel the truth in those words all the way to my soul.

CHAPTER FORTY TWO

GAVIN

"I thought you left," I whisper, my voice sounding like someone else.

"You thought wrong. I did borrow your truck though."

"Where did you go?"

"First to Jules' house because I have some stuff and money there. Then, I went and picked you up some things."

"Moonbeam, I hurt too fucking much to eat."

"I get that, Baby. I do. But I got some pain pills and if you're going to take one of those, you have to eat a little something."

"Tylenol won't hurt on an empty—"

"It's not Tylenol. I got you the good stuff from when I had my wisdom teeth out."

"You—"

"I had a few left and I keep them at Jules' for when I'm there and my monthly crap gets really bad."

"You have that much trouble? I've never noticed."

"I keep that hidden from you, Gav. I don't want you to see me like that."

"Don't do that anymore," I mutter, taking the water she hands me and downing a couple of the pills.

"Do what?"

"Hide things from me. If you're hurting, I want to know. I want to help."

"There's not much you can do in that case, Gavin."

"Maybe not, but I can try. I can be there," I add, then stop because I start coughing and son of a bitch if that doesn't hurt like hell.

"Stop growling at me, it's causing you pain."

I want to argue with her, but I can't. "You should probably head back home. Your parents will send out a search party for you soon."

"My parents can go to hell."

"Luna, you don't mean that."

"I do," she insists and then she starts cleaning the cut near my mouth with some alcohol. I hiss from the burn of pain. "Sorry, Baby," she murmurs, blowing on the wound. Even in pain, it feels nice. I can't remember anyone ever giving a damn about me. This with Luna… it's good.

Really good.

"Three babies in one night, I've hit the motherlode," I joke.

Her face looks confused for a minute, but then she understands and shakes her head at me.

"You're crazy. Anyway, I'm done listening to my parents. They've been lying to me for months. All this crap about wanting someone good for me, someone that will treat me good and not even giving you a chance."

"Luna—"

"And it was all lies. *Especially* from my father. How can he preach about me finding a good man to treat me like I deserve when he's cheating on my mom and practically living with another woman?"

"Fuck. That's rough."

"That's one word for it."

"Your mom must be a mess."

"Yeah, she is, but she lied to me. She should have told me the truth."

"She's probably going through hell right now, Moonbeam. I'd say she was just trying to shield you for as long as she could."

"Maybe, but that doesn't make it any better."

"Yeah."

"Anyway, I called her from Jules' and told her I need a break. They won't be sending any search parties out tonight."

"That's good. I'd rather not deal with your dad tonight."

"You and me both, but he's not an issue since he left for the Hamptons and back to his mistress."

"Fuck, Luna—"

"It's okay, Gavin. I'm okay. It's just what I needed to make me realize something."

"What's that?"

"That you're my home. We'll leave after graduation and we'll start our own place in the world."

"You mean that," I whisper, suddenly feeling better than I have in years, despite the pain.

"I'm completely serious."

"God, I love you," I tell her, leaning down to kiss her, and I press our lips hard together, despite the pain, thrusting my tongue in her mouth and kissing her with all of the hunger I have for her.

When we break apart, I rest my forehead against her as my heart rate slowly comes down to normal.

"I love you. I do have a small favor to ask you, however."

"Anything," I promise.

"You don't even know what I'm going to ask," she laughs.

"It doesn't matter. I'll find a way to give you the world if you wanted it."

"Silly. All I want is you, Gavin Lodge."

"You have me, Moonbeam. You always will."

"I'm counting on that," she murmurs softly, our gazes locked on one another, and I can see the love radiating on her face.

Love for me.

"What was your favor?" I ask.

"Can we go back to Jules and spend the weekend there? She's kind of freaked out, even though she won't admit it."

"Why? What's happened?"

"There was another murder. This time in Russell."

"Shit."

"Same scenario. Found the girl naked, her hands were bound this time and apparently, it's not a black rose they found like Jules has been getting, but a blood rose, which is even creepier. It's a white rose with splashes of red that look like blood."

"Well, that's good for Jules though, right?"

"I guess. But she got a note today and she hadn't read it until she got home. She thought it was just another annoying note the guy has been putting in her locker. Instead, it told her to watch the news."

"And?"

"She did. That's how she found out about the second murder."

"Fuck. Did she call the cops?"

"She did, but they told her it was probably just a prank. They did promise to do some patrols in her neighborhood and asked to talk to her parents, but of course..."

"Her parents are gone for the weekend."

"Let's load up."

"Are you up to it?"

"Yeah, you'll probably have to drive, but I'll survive."

"We don't have to, Gavin."

"We do, Moonbeam. Your girl needs people around her and besides, if there is some freak on the loose just the next town over, the last thing I want is for you to be out in the open all night."

"If you're sure."

"Yeah, just one thing."

"What's that?" she asks.

"Help me up." I sigh, feeling weak as water and hating that I need help to do anything.

"You got it, Baby," she says with a grin, pressing a gentle kiss on my cheek.

Maybe needing help isn't such a bad thing....

CHAPTER FORTY THREE

LUNA

"It's about time you got home," Dad growls as soon as I walk through the door.

"I spent the night at Jules' house," I tell him, barely bothering to look up. If he thinks I care what he has to say at this point, he's crazy. "Besides, I thought you left us again… *on business*—right?"

"That's it, Luna. You're grounded. There will be no going to Jules' house. There will be nothing but school and home for you, young lady."

"Are you seriously starting this shit on me?"

"Since when is it okay for you to curse, Luna Ann Marshall?"

"Oh, I don't know since you failed to recognize that I'll be eighteen in a couple of weeks?"

"You still live under my roof!"

"No, I don't. You have a new family now, Dad. Remember?"

"Quit being sarcastic, Luna. It doesn't become you."

I look at the man I used to love with everything inside of me. The man I still love, but also hate a little. I look at the man that I used to think hung the moon. He doesn't look like my superhero now. He doesn't even look like my dad. If he wasn't trying to ground me and be a complete asshole, I'd almost feel sorry for him. Then, I look over at my mother and see how her eyes are swollen, take in the fact that she's been crying. While I'm looking at her, I notice for the first time that she's lost a lot of weight. She's been living in hell and I didn't even know. Any sympathy I had for my father dissipates.

"Quit trying to be a father, that doesn't become you either."

"I am your father, Luna."

"Your new woman, does she have kids, Dad?"

I hear Mom's gasp and I hate that I'm causing her pain. I'm not happy with her right now, but it's clear she's hurting too. I wish she had told me. All this time that she's been crying, she could have told me. Instead, she let me be blindsided.

"Does she?" I persist.

I watch as he rubs the back of his neck in irritation and his face looks bleak.

"She does. A girl about your age. I'd like for you guys to meet soon."

"Do they know about me? Dad? Do they know about my Mom?"

"Luna?"

"Did they? When you were cheating with this woman, did she know about us? Did she have any idea what she was tearing apart? Did she know who she was hurting?"

"Luna—"

"Answer me!" I scream, pain lancing through me, because I know the answer.

"She knew your mother and I were separated," he finally says.

"But...you weren't—not really. Your clothes were still hanging in the closet. You still came home on the weekends. You still pretended everything was fine. So, you lied to her too. You've lied to *everyone*." I shake my head as all the hurt and lies swirl around in my head enough to make me dizzy.

"I'm not getting into this with you right now, Luna. You'll find out when you become an adult that things aren't always so black and white."

"I think I'm more of an adult than you are. I'm adult enough to know that when you love someone you try to help them and protect them, not hurt them."

"Don't think I don't know what this is about, Luna."

"What's it about, Dad?"

"Your little infatuation with that Lodge boy."

"It's not an infatuation, I love him, Dad. And I doubt anyone in the history of ever has referred to Gavin as a boy."

"You're too young to know what love is. I refuse to let you ruin your life over some kid who will never amount to a damn thing."

"You don't know anything about Gavin. You didn't even give him a chance!"

"I know that he'll probably end up just like his father, the town drunk and without a dime to his name. I'm not about to let you throw your life away on someone like him."

"Gavin's nothing like his dad!"

His words are as harsh as the expression on his grim face. "Not yet. Give him time."

"He loves me. He'd never hurt me. He works almost thirty hours a week and still goes to school. He's nothing like his father."

"I'm not arguing with you about this, Luna. You're not seeing that Lodge boy. That's final. And until you learn to be civil to me, you're grounded."

"No, she's not," Mom says.

"I've had enough of your mouth—" Dad stops talking once he finally hears what Mom said. He jerks his head around to look at her. "What are you talking about, Lydia?"

"Luna's not grounded. She's under *my* roof now, not yours. She called me to tell me she was going to Jules. She didn't hide it, and I trust my daughter. She's not grounded."

"It's going to be like that," Dad says, narrowing his eyes at Mom, clearly not happy.

Her shoulders straighten. "Exactly like that, Arthur."

"Good luck keeping the roof over your head, then. If you want to play hardball, Lydia, then I can too."

"Oh, I'll keep the roof over my head, Arthur. It will be fairly easy."

"I doubt that. You've not bothered to even try and hold a job down in years."

"I won't now either. You'll make sure everything is paid."

"You're dreaming. I'll help with Luna, but she'll be eighteen and—"

"It's called alimony, Arthur and you're loaded, while I've been the naïve, doting wife who dropped out and worked to send you through school to achieve your dream, had your child, and later did everything for you, right down to drawing your bathwater and laying your clothes out for the next day."

Dad doesn't respond. His face goes hard and that's when I see the real man clearly. Not a hero… just a man and someone I'm not sure I ever really knew. My idea of him was a fantasy.

"I'm going to go upstairs. I have a final to study for," I murmur, walking away. The oxygen is way too thick in the room and suddenly I need air desperately.

"You're still not to see that Lodge boy, Luna," Dad warns me. I stop at the bottom of the stairs and look back at him, about to tell him that it's not up to him when Mom responds.

"He's right on this, Luna."

"Mom—"

"You don't need to throw your life away on a boy—any boy. You need to go to school and get an education."

"I can still have that—"

"Go to school. Get a career you can be proud of, stand on your own two feet, Luna."

I want to argue more, but I see from the way she is looking at me, she's too lost in her own hurt to listen. She's also close to breaking. I need to pick my battles and right now, there's no way I can win this one. Eventually, I'll make Mom understand that Gavin is not like Dad. Gavin would never lie, and he wouldn't hurt me. Today is clearly not the day to prove that. Gavin won't like that we're still hiding, but he'll be okay with it. We'll be leaving Stone Lake behind soon and starting our lives together.

That's all that matters.

CHAPTER FORTY FOUR

ATTICUS

"Are you fucking my brother?"

Jules eyes go wide at my question as she leans against the door.

"Attie, I don't have time for your bullshit tonight. I've got too much on my plate."

"Answer me, Jules. I'm not playing with you."

"But, Attie, I like it when you play with me," she replies coyly. She takes a step into my body and drags a fingernail down the side of my face. She thinks it's cute. I find it annoying as hell. Though if she wants to play, I can play. I grab her hair and yank it so hard she cries out. I twist it and use the hold to pull her face close. My other hand wraps around her throat. I can feel the muscles move under my palm as she swallows. I can almost smell her fear, and I get hard from that alone. Of all of the bitches I've been dealing with lately, Jules gets me going like none of the others.

"I'm going to ask you one more time and you're going to answer me, Jules. Do you understand me?"

"Damn it, Attie!"

I growl, moving my hand up and slapping it hard against her

mouth. Her voice is annoying the shit out of me right now. Actually, Jules herself is bothering me. I swear I can smell my brother on her.

Her eyes go round, the pupils dilating. I feel her breath release in harsh puffs against my hand and she tries to nod her head yes. I know that causes her pain because of the way I'm holding her. The realization makes me smile.

"I'm not playing games with you, Jules. I'm not some dog you can play with and then kick for the hell of it, either. Are we clear?"

She nods her head again, tears gathering in the corner of her eyes.

"Good. Now that we have that straight. Be a good girl and answer my question. *Are you fucking my brother?"*

I pronounce each word of my question separately, taking a breath in between each one to help control my anger. I can accept her fucking Darren Oakes. I couldn't give two shits about that. I will not take her fucking Gavin. It's bad enough that Luna is all wound up around the bastard. She'll soon see how stupid she's been, but I will not let this little cock tease throw me aside for my brother. I take my hand away from her mouth and wait for her to answer me.

"I'm not," she says her voice hoarse and shaking a little.

She's afraid.

Good. She should be.

"What was he doing here?" I question further, refusing to let her go.

"Luna was here."

"You've been helping them see each other," I surmise, letting her go.

She stumbles as she steps away from me.

"Yeah," she says, rubbing her mouth. Jules watches me closely and she's dripping in fear now. It's good she knows she can't play with me.

"I don't like that."

"I don't like you hitting me."

"Liar."

"I'm serious, Attie. That's not cool," she says, starting to get a little braver, but she is still talking quietly, as if she's afraid to set me off.

She should be afraid.

"We both know you love it when I'm rough with you, Jules." I smirk.

"Not like that, and not right now," she denies.

"What's different about right now? Is your new boy toy here?"

"No. I… Attie I think that Blood Rose Killer is the one sending me notes."

"The ones you've been talking about? He hasn't threatened you in them, though."

"No, but this last one told me to watch the news and there was another murder on it… I'm scared, Attie."

"Did you tell your parents?"

"Yeah, but they won't listen. They don't give a damn. Their weekends are all about going to their damn swinging parties. They don't give a fuck about me," she says, looking wounded. Like a little bird with clipped wings.

I don't think it's my imagination that I see pain on her face. It's a pain I'm familiar with, because I know what it means when your parents don't give a fuck if you live or die. Maybe that's why I connect with Jules so much—well that and she's as twisted up inside as I am.

"You're probably overreacting, Jules. He hasn't been sending notes to the other girls. Right? They've not mentioned anything about that on the news. It's just someone fucking with you."

"Then, how did they know to tell me to watch the news, Einstein?"

"Maybe they didn't? Have you seen the shit on the news? Odds are if it hadn't been the murder something else would have caught your eye on the news. Maybe there was a story about a guy putting flowers in the lockers of the prettiest girls in the local schools."

"There wasn't," she says with a resigned sigh. Then she gives me a small smile that doesn't quite reach her eyes. "You think I'm pretty?"

"I wouldn't let you have my dick if I didn't."

"That's so sweet, Attie," she teases, rolling her eyes.

"That's me... *sweet.*"

"No, it's not. You're a jerk. My mouth hurts, you asshole," she grumbles, moving a finger over her bottom lip.

"Let me inside, and I'll give you something to make your mouth feel better," I promise, with a smile.

"I'm not in the mood to sleep with you, Attie," she tells me coolly.

"That's good, we're not going to sleep."

"*Idiot.*"

"I can leave and find someone else who is not nearly as good at sucking me off as you."

"Gee, again with the sweet talk."

"But that would leave you alone with some serial killer out there... or I could come in..."

"Fine, dick-wad, come inside, but no more hitting. I might like it a little rough but hitting is not my thing."

"Fine, no hitting. You just like choking..."

"You really are an asshole," she mutters as I go inside.

She closes the door behind me and starts to walk away. I grab her hand and stop her from leaving. She looks at me in surprise. I capture her gaze and pointedly look at the door, before turning the lever on the deadbolt and locking the door.

"Wouldn't want anyone to hurt you," I tell her, and her face softens.

"Let's go upstairs, Attie," she says, tugging on my hand. I let her take the lead.

Besides... I like watching her ass...

CHAPTER FORTY FIVE

GAVIN

"Do you like it?" I ask Luna when she does nothing more than stare at the box.

Until Luna, I've never had a girl in my life that I wanted to get a gift for, so I have no idea if I did this right. I mean, she seemed to like the locket I got her for Christmas. Maybe I should have gotten her jewelry again. I thought she would like this, but what if I'm wrong?

"It's a photo album..."

"Yeah," I mumble, thinking now that I hear it out loud it does sound pretty lame. Doesn't make it better that she keeps staring at it.

"And cameras."

"Disposable ones... each one takes like thirty pictures, though. So, that's like a hundred and fifty pictures..."

"I—"

"I should have bought you a real camera. I was trying to save money for when we leave Stone Lake, but I mean it's your birthday and I suck. Shit, Luna, I'm sorry," I apologize, embarrassment coloring me. Hell, I can even feel heat travel up my face.

"Gavin—"

"I just thought we could take pictures of our life together. Something to record every moment of the life we build. I never really had pictures. I can barely remember what my mom looked like before she left us. I always thought that if I managed to build a life that I was proud of, I'd want to make sure I had the memory of it around me."

"Gavin—"

"It's stupid, I guess. But, you're a girl, so I figured you'd enjoy that too. Christ. Let's just forget it. How about I take you out tonight to Romano's for spaghetti. It's a ritzy place. You can get all dressed up. Heck, wear your prom dress early. We can—"

"Gavin! Stop interrupting me," Luna yells and I jerk my face down to look at her.

"I love the photo album and the cameras."

"Come on, Luna, you don't have to lie. Girls don't stare at something for an hour if they like it."

"I didn't stare for an hour. And, I just... Seeing the gift made me realize something."

"What?"

"We'll be leaving Stone Lake in a little over a month."

"Fuck yeah we will. I can't wait."

"You won't miss it? Not even a little?"

"There's nothing here that means anything to me, Luna. Nothing but you and you'll be with me." She smiles and leans up to kiss me and I meet her, taking a deeper taste of her mouth. When we break apart, I study her face. I ignore my nervousness as a thought hits me. "You're not having second thoughts, are you?"

"No. Not about being with you, Gavin. I just... I'm worried about my mom."

"She'll be okay, Luna. And we can still come back and see her. I promise."

"I know. She seems so sad all the time."

"I know, Babe, but she'll get back on her feet again. This is her life and she's got to live it—just like you need to live yours."

"You're right. I know you are, I'm just worried."

"What if we wait until June to head out? That way you're here for your mom when the divorce becomes final."

"You'd be willing to do that?"

"I don't like it, but it's only a couple weeks. If it will make you feel better, then, I'm fine with it."

"I still can't believe that they'll be divorced so quickly."

"Well, it helped that your dad agreed to your mom's terms, you know? Like, once he agreed to sign the paper her attorney drew up, it was pretty much over then."

"I guess, it just seems like a marriage that lasted twenty-five years should be harder to undo..."

"I'm sorry, Moonbeam."

"Me too. I can't imagine what Mom is feeling."

"You'll never have to know."

"Gavin," she whispers, looking at me.

"I promise you, Luna. I'll never cheat on you; never hurt you like that. I know you love your dad, but that was a fucking horrible thing to do to your mom. No one ever deserves to be hurt like that," I tell her.

I take her into my arms, pulling her backwards so we're lying on the dock, looking up at the sky.

"I'm scared, Gavin."

"Why, Moonbeam?"

"Everything is changing so fast... Everything I've ever known is wrong."

"We're not wrong."

"My parents loved each other once. Now they hate each other."

"That will never happen to us, Luna."

"How can you be sure?"

"I just know. I know when I look in your eyes."

"How?"

"It sounds like a line, but it's not."

"What does?"

"When I look in your eyes, Luna… I just know that everything I am ever going to want in life is staring back at me."

"If it is a line, it's a really good one," she murmurs.

"It's the God's honest truth, Moonbeam," I swear.

"Gavin, shut up and kiss me."

I take the camera from her hand and hold it up in front of us. I have no idea if we'll even be in the frame, but I snap it as I kiss her.

It seems like a great picture to begin our story with….

CHAPTER FORTY SIX

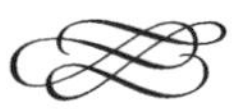

GAVIN

"Don't stop, Gavin," Luna moans in my ear.

I'm fast approaching the point where I can't hold back. Luna and I have experimented some, but she wasn't ready for sex and I've never pushed her. It's been hard not to go all the way, but we've talked about it and Luna just hasn't been ready to take that step. I'm not about to push her, because Luna is more than sex. I told her we had the rest of our lives together, that we didn't need to push things, and I was completely serious.

That doesn't mean my balls don't hate me.

They seem to be living in a constant state of blue.

It also doesn't mean nights like tonight aren't hard. I'm dying to have her—so hungry that my body feels like it is being tortured. Hearing her plead for more serves in making it worse. Luna is innocent. She has no idea what she does to me beyond the obvious signs.

A hoarse growl escapes as her hand wraps around my hard cock.

"Luna, you're playing with fire," I warn her, my fingers sliding against her heated flesh. She's so wet that it would be easy to push inside of her. I shake with the need to do that, but instead I settle for moving the pads of my fingers around the swollen nub that's pulsing in hunger.

This is as far as we've gone. Always before she's pulled back, stopped us before we crossed that line that would be impossible to come back from.

"I don't care, Gavin. I don't want to wait. I'm tired of waiting. I want to belong to you."

"Luna," I moan, my control so close to snapping as her hand slides up and down my shaft, stroking me. Her hand is heaven, but what would it be like to be inside her hot, wet, tight pussy?

What would it be like to take her virginity and make her come all over my cock?

The mere thought makes my body shake with need.

"I want you to take me, Gavin. I don't want to wait anymore. We're going away together. You said we belong to each other. There's no point in waiting anymore. I need you."

Damn it.

It'd be so easy to give in. To give her—to give both of us—what we want.

"Luna," I whisper into her ear. "Give me your mouth."

She doesn't even question. Suddenly her lips are on mine. Her tongue searches mine, hungrily and unpracticed, completely lost to passion and I'm there with her. Our tongues mate, and I kiss her with all the love I have inside of me—it all belongs to her anyway. Her shirt is gone, lying on the floor with her pants. That leaves her bra on, and my hand down inside of her panties. Luna has been shy, afraid to be naked in front of me. She's never let anyone see her in the nude before, and I like that. I like that I am the first man she's loved. I like that I will be her first lover, her first orgasm, all of it. I hate that we keep her underwear on when we make out, but I know eventually they will come off. I've already had her bra off, but only in the dark and even then, she blushed so deeply that I think she was glowing in the darkness.

I haven't minded any of it, even though Luna is scared I have. She feels pressure because all of her friends are having sex. The thing is, Luna makes me feel like no one ever has. Things with her are special. Hell, at this point I can't imagine being with anyone but her. I never want to make love with anyone else.

Just Luna.

Always Luna.

That doesn't mean I don't despise her panties. I hate them and one day very soon—when we're sleeping together every night—I will forbid her to come to bed with clothes on. If she tries, I'll rip them off of her. I live for that day.

But now is now.

And we've always made sure her panties stayed on—a thin barrier that managed somehow to keep me sane and from taking her even when my body was screaming for me to do so. I want to rip them off now, but I still find myself holding back, despite her plea.

Hell, maybe after a year and a half of just doing this with Luna, I'm the one scared to push for more, afraid she'll run away.

So, instead, my hand is busy at work inside of her panties. I slide my fingers, which are covered in her arousal, back and forth over her clit. It's not enough for Luna, and I know that when she thrusts up against my hand, trying to grind. One of her legs wraps around one of mine and she tries to pull my body against hers—does her best to get us closer.

"Gavin, stop torturing me," she whimpers, her hand stroking me harder.

Pre-cum runs down my shaft, over her hand, making my cock slick. She's jacking me so tightly, her hand clenching as she gets closer to the edge. I let out a ragged breath that ends in a hiss as I feel my balls tighten.

I'm going to come. I can't hold back.

I break away from her mouth and use my nose and teeth to nudge her bra out of the way, all the while torturing her clit with my fingers. I want to fuck her with my fingers, but I won't even allow myself that. When I claim her virginity, I want to do it with my cock, not my hand. I have no idea if that is possible, but I've heard guys say it is and I don't want to risk it. Fuck, the truth is I'm not much more experienced than Luna—mostly because from the moment I first saw her, no other girl would do.

It's always been her.

"I'm going to come, Moonbeam," I whisper in her ear, my voice coarse, threaded with hunger and almost unrecognizable.

"No," she whimpers, as I pick up my speed and the intensity on the way I'm working her clit.

She's so wet now that she has my hand drenched. Her body is thrusting against me, making movements that I doubt she understands, but even in my limited experience, I know. She needs more than I'm giving her. We'll have to talk about it, but I need her to make the decision when she's not on the verge of coming, when she's not hungry and needy.

"Come for me, Luna. Give in and let me make it all better," I croon, before dropping my head back down to her breast.

I lick around the nipple, and as her body jerks underneath me I suck the tender bud into my mouth, thrusting it against the top of my mouth and torturing it. My free hand teases the other breast, working her up to the point that I know she'll explode.

She strokes me, her hand unpracticed and the rhythm is broken at times, but it feels so damn good, my eyes close against the sweetness of it. I hold on, even though it's not easy. I need to make sure she comes first.

She will always come first.

"Gavin," she cries, her body going tense, her hand squeezing my cock so tight it's painful.

I open my eyes, watching as her orgasm overtakes her, hurling her over the edge. I watch every moment of it. Kissing her breast, kissing up her chest, her neck along the angles of her face, everywhere I can, my fingers slowing down, stroking her clit and carefully bringing her back to earth.

Cherishing her. Loving her.

She's everything.

CHAPTER FORTY SEVEN

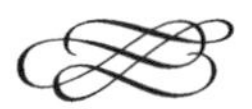

LUNA

When my eyes finally open, I find Gavin staring at me intently. The deep blue of his are shimmering with a passion that sears me.

"That's not what I wanted." My voice is soft, my voice deeper than normal and I can hear the pleasure in it. I know Gavin can too.

"I know," he admits.

I've kept my hand on his cock, even though I'm not moving. His hand is pressed against my center and I know proof of my climax is pooling against his palm, but I'm not embarrassed—at least not as much as I used to be.

This is Gavin.

I'm safe.

"Then, why didn't you... *you know?*"

His mouth moves into a small smile and he leans down kissing my lips just briefly.

"Moonbeam—"

"Don't you want me, Gavin?" I ask quietly, voicing my biggest fear.

"Don't be crazy, Luna."

"I'm serious. We've been together for a long time now. I gave you the go ahead, guys are supposed to…" I stop talking, blushing so deeply in color that the heat washes over my body. I don't know what else to say, I'm feeling uncomfortable and more than a little stupid.

"Babe, we've talked about this. You're not just some quick lay to me. Until you're ready, I can wait."

"Gavin—"

"Luna, I'd wait forever for you."

"I just…"

"Your hand is on my cock, Luna. You feel how hard I am right now. You have to know how much I want you."

"Then, why didn't you?"

He rolls over on his back and looks up at the ceiling. I feel bad, afraid that I ruined the moment.

"I'm sorry, Gavin. I'm just being silly," I tell him, draping half over him, my hand going to his face. I put a little pressure on it, trying to bring his gaze back to mine.

"Luna, if you knew how much I wanted you, it would probably terrify you."

"But—"

"I didn't take it farther with you, because I refuse to take your virginity while we're in your friend's bed, and I don't get to hold you all night long."

"Oh…"

"You're special, Babe, and I haven't waited all this time to not make it special for you when it happens. If you're sure that you're ready to take the next step, then we'll plan, and I'll make sure I have everything in place to take care of you."

"Everything in place?"

"Condoms, Luna. I don't have any tonight."

"Oh, crap."

"I'm not going to risk getting you pregnant," he says adamantly.

"I like babies."

"Right now, you having a child is the absolute worst thing that could happen."

"Gavin—"

"I'm serious, Luna. We're going to be leaving everything behind. I'll have some money saved up, but not a lot. We'll have to make it stretch until we have a regular income coming in. I think I can find a job pretty easily, but still it will be hard for the first couple of months and even then, it will be harder than anything you've been used to in your life."

"I'm not stupid, Gavin. I know it will be hard, but I will work too. You don't have to do everything on your own."

"I know that, Moonbeam. I'm just saying there's no way a baby will fit into our plans."

"Yeah, I mean I've just turned eighteen, I'm not ready to be a mom for sure, but…"

"But, what?"

"You do want kids someday, don't you?"

"I never really thought about it. I think once I would have said no way…"

"But, not now?"

"Now? After you? Loving you? It'd be a shame if you didn't pass all that love on to a child."

I place a kiss on his chest, letting my fingers move over his stomach as I stare into his blue eyes. "I love you," I respond, not sure of what else to say, my heart feeling way too full.

"But kids are something we should think about and plan, Moonbeam. I want to get us settled. I'd like to have a career that will support us, a home—a nice one like the one you live in."

"Gavin, I'm not waiting that long to belong to you. I want you to be my first."

"You're crazy if I'd let anyone else claim you, Luna. You're mine. I'm going to be your first and last. We're going to last *forever*."

"I like the sound of that."

"I'm serious. If we have problems, we talk them out. We learn from the mistakes our parents have made."

"Okay, so when? Because, I have to warn you, Gavin, if you don't make love to me soon, I'm going to catch you sleeping and attack you." He laughs, as I intended him to do, but I'm not really joking either.

"How about prom?"

"Prom? Isn't that a tad cliché?" I laugh, my body warming at the heated look in his eyes.

"Maybe but ask me if I give a fuck? Your mom already thinks you'll be staying over at the all-night party the school is having afterward. We'll check in and then sneak out. I'll take things from there."

"You're serious?"

"Oh, yeah." He grins and I frown at him. "What's wrong?" he asks, confused.

"Prom is like two weeks away," I whine. "I don't want to wait that long."

"Do you want my hand again? Or, I could give you my mouth."

"Your mouth?" My body tingles by the promise of that. I've always felt uncomfortable around boys. Gavin's not just any boy. I love him, but still, it's scary thinking about standing in front of him naked, baring myself to him.

What if he doesn't like me? What if I'm not as pretty as the girls he's used to?

Everyone I know is having sex. It seems to be all they think about. I've never been like that. If it wasn't for my all-consuming attraction for Gavin Lodge, I'd worry I am as cold as the whole student body jokes that I am.

"Oh yeah. Do you want me to show you how good I can make you feel?"

My body screams yes, but when I look at the boy that I love more than anything in the world, there's something I want more.

"I know something I want even more."

"What's that, Moonbeam? You know that I'd give you anything I could," he says, sitting up and leaning against the headboard. I move with him so I'm half-sitting, still draped over his body. His hand moves to the side of my neck, his thumb brushing against my jawline and sweeping to my chin.

"I want to watch."

"Watch?" he asks, his face showing his confusion. It clears up quickly though, when I wrap my hand around his still hard cock and start stroking him.

"I want to watch you as you come," I confess, my voice so quiet that he probably has to strain to hear me.

It might be lame, I have no idea. But, always before, I've been so caught up in what Gavin was doing to me to notice his face, his actions when he came. I saw the pleasure on his face afterwards. I saw the lazy smile and the happiness in his eyes, but I missed the during. Suddenly, I want to see that more than anything else in the world.

"Moonbeam," he moans, his head going back as I hold him solidly in my hand, stroking him in the steady rhythm that he's taught me. Until Gavin, I've never even experimented or played around. He's had to teach me everything. I have no idea, it might be annoying to him, but I love it. I love that he is teaching me exactly what he likes.

"Look at me, Gavin. Let me watch you," I beg.

He raises his head back up, his gaze locked on me. His face tightens with hunger, and I lick my lips seeing the desire overtake him.

"Take your bra off, Luna."

A thrill moves through me, closely followed by panic. I remind myself that this is Gavin—that I am safe with him. I reach behind and unlatch my bra. I catch the front before it falls completely. I take a breath and then let it fall. I can feel heat blossom over my face, but I fight it down. I take his cock back in my hand, my movements not as sure as earlier. Gavin puts his hand over mine, steadying me, and teaching me how to curl my hand with each thrust. Slowly we pick up speed. Gavin's watching my breasts, his eyes heavy-lidded. I follow his gaze, seeing how my breasts sway with each of the strokes. Slowly, I look back at him and I can see the exact moment it hits him. His head goes back as he groans, his body trembles.

He's beautiful.

My hand which was already slick is now covered as streams of his cum jets out, splashing against my hand and even splattering against my breasts. He watches, the heat from his gaze burning me.

"Mine," he whispers.

And I am…

CHAPTER FORTY EIGHT

GAVIN

"You sure about this, Jules?"

"Yeah, no problem. I'm going to be here all night unless I convince Darren to go to the frat party in Hagerstown. So, it's no biggie."

"I can get a hotel room…"

"You know as well as I do the minute you and Luna walk into the Holiday Inn, which is the only decent hotel here in Stone Lake, someone would call Luna's mom immediately."

"Yeah, probably. I could take her to Russell or even Monroe, but…"

"Stop already. It's fine. The house will be empty. The parental units flew out to Vegas for their wild party. They won't be back until Tuesday. I won't be home until Sunday afternoon, which means you have the place all to yourselves tonight."

"I appreciate it, I want to make this perfect for Luna."

She smirks at me. "You really love her, don't you?"

"Luna means everything to me," I tell her truthfully.

"If I didn't know it before, I'd know it now. You must have bought out the flower shop."

I can't be sure, but I think I blush when I look at the eight dozen roses I bought. I also got candles, bath oils, and a CD of Luna's favorite band.

"I just want her to be happy."

"Do you think she will be, leaving Stone Lake behind?"

"I think I'm going to do everything in my power to make her happy," I hedge, hating her questions because that's my biggest worry.

"Of everyone I know, Luna loves it here. Me? Hell, I'd be happier anywhere but here and as far away from my fucking parents as I can get. Luna has never been that way."

"I know, but I'm going to give her everything I can so that she doesn't miss Stone Lake."

"What if what she wants most is for you to stay in Stone Lake with her?" Jules asks.

I frown, unease welling up in my stomach. I would do anything for Luna—absolutely anything. I am scared that I'd even try to stay here, if that's what would make her happy. Luna is my lifeline, but she could easily become an anchor, holding me down in the one place that I'm desperate to leave far behind. If it comes down to choosing Luna over leaving Stone Lake?

Will I be able to choose?

I haven't told Luna, but life with my father has only gotten worse. I beat the shit out of him a couple of days ago and last night I woke up to him holding a lighter over my bed, flicking it on and off repeatedly. Atticus was snoring, he didn't even know. My father didn't say a word, but I knew what the message meant.

It's sobering to realize that your father, the man who is responsible for you breathing air would just as soon kill you as to look at you. Sometimes I wonder why he hasn't yet....

"I can see you're struggling with that one," she says, and I look up to see her watching me closely.

"There are things..."

"Yeah, I know. Attie has told me some of it."

"I didn't realize you and Atticus were that close."

"There's a lot about me that you don't know, Gav. I'm mysterious like that. Listen, I'm heading over to my girl's house to get prettied up for the prom. Here's the key to the front door. I left you a bottle of wine chilling. You're welcome, by the way," she adds tossing me the key.

"Thanks, Jules" I say on a laugh, catching it.

Jules is completely different than Luna, but I can see why Luna loves her. Once you get through her walls and bitchiness, she really cares, and she really loves Luna—that much is clear.

"No problem-o. Just make sure you bring enough raincoats to the party. You don't want to run short of those."

I roll my eyes, not about to answer that. Jules doesn't care, she leaves without a backwards glance. I gather all the roses and head upstairs. I need to set the scene here and get in that ridiculous tux for the prom.

I hope Luna is okay with leaving that early....

CHAPTER FORTY NINE

LUNA

"Boy, Attie, you clean up nice."

"Thanks," he mutters, looking uncomfortable. "I still can't believe you got my brother to show up to this thing."

"I'd do anything for Luna," Gavin says coming back and handing me a glass of punch. I take a drink and curl my nose.

"What is this crap?"

"I'm not sure, but I think it's straight up pineapple juice and fruit cocktail," Attie says.

"Gross."

"Sorry, Babe, I fetch the punch, I don't make it."

"It's good Luna's at least teaching you to fetch," Atticus replies, and I see Gavin's face harden at his brother's snarky reply.

"Attie—"

"Let it go, Moonbeam. He's not worth the trouble," Gavin mutters.

I lean back, my head against his chest and position my head so I can see his face. Gavin gives me a smile and bends down and kisses my forehead.

"Is Attie causing trouble again?" Jules laughs, coming up beside us.

"Just the normal," Attie replies with a shrug. "Your date finally let you out of his sight?"

"Jealous?"

"Not at all," Atticus replies drolly.

"Whatever. Where's Candy Bishop?"

"She'll be back shortly."

"I can't believe you're dating that whore," Jules mutters.

"I can't believe *you're* calling her a whore."

Jules narrows her eyes at him, and I can tell she's about to light into him, because his hidden meaning was very clear. I don't know what it is about these two anymore, but they always throw digs at one another.

"Can't we all just get along?" I mumble.

"No." Everyone around me says it practically at the same time and I simply hold my head down in defeat which makes Jules laugh.

"Oh, cool it, Luna. You're just happy because you and Gavin are about to head out together for the *whole* night."

I blush. I can't help it. Gavin's arm tightens around me.

"Can it, Jules," he warns, and she rolls her eyes at him.

"Just make sure you clean my house when you're done having wild virgin monkey sex." she laughs. "I'm out of here." She walks off, stumbling slightly.

"She's drunk," I tell them. "Maybe I should insist on taking her home.

"I'll see to her," Atticus says.

"No, I will. I—"

"I got this, Luna," Atticus growls and walks away.

"This was not how I envisioned prom," I mumble at Gavin.

"Told you, Moonbeam, prom is lame."

"I guess so," I agree, completely disappointed.

"Of course, I have the prettiest girl here and that pale pink dress you're wearing is slowly killing me, so I can deal with lame."

"Killing you?" I laugh as he takes me into his arms.

"The thing is cut so low in the back that every time you walk, I know it's going to dip down and flash that cute little beauty mark above your ass."

"Is that why you keep walking behind me?"

"Well, I do that so no one else can see that ass but me, but if I can see that mark for myself? That's just a bonus."

"What do you say we head out early and you can have an up close and personal encounter with said mark?" I ask, ignoring the heat on my face.

"You sure?"

"Definitely."

"What about the chances of your mom calling and finding out you're not where you're supposed to be?"

I try to keep the sadness out of my expression, and I give Gavin a small smile, that feels more bitter than anything.

"When I left, she was sleeping off a bottle of wine. I think we're safe."

"I'm sorry, Moonbeam."

"It is what it is," I tell him, hating that my life has changed so drastically.

"Then, let's leave and maybe I can make some of it better."

"You always make everything better, Gavin. *Always.*"

He leans down and kisses, me taking my hand in his and we walk toward the exit. I'm nervous as a cat, but I'm excited too.

Tonight is the night.

Tonight I will finally make love to Gavin.

CHAPTER FIFTY

ATTICUS

"Your date seems to be getting awful close to Meghan Flint."

"They're just dancing, Attie," Jules responds, downing the rest of her drink.

"What are you drinking?"

"Just punch."

"Yeah, right. If that's punch, then I'm the King of England."

"If that's true, then England is doo…" she breaks off to hiccup. "…oomed."

I reach over and take her drink.

"Hey give that back," she cries.

"It's empty," I remind her.

"Oh. I'll have to get another one," she says with a sigh looking around.

"You need to lay off of it. You're wasted, Jules."

"So? What does it matter? You don't care, neither does Darren. My parents sure as hell don't care. About the only person that's ever gave a damn about me is Luna and she's too busy all up in Gavin's ass to worry about me."

"Poor little rich girl," I snarl, sick of Jules' attitude. She has it made and doesn't even appreciate it.

"Fuck you, Atticus," she seethes, but it would carry more conviction if she wasn't drunk off her ass and her head wasn't lolling to the front at an odd angle. I think I even see drool leaking from the side of her mouth.

"You're such a bitch. You have it made. You're all poor pitiful me and why? Because your parents set you up in a killer house with a pool, pay your bills, buy you a car, and give you your own fucking credit card? You're pathetic."

"You don't know anything about my life!" she yells standing up, but she doesn't quite make it because her dress gets tangled up in her chair and she falls back down.

"I know you have it made. You're just feeling sorry for yourself because your parents are never around to dote attention on you, like the princess you try to pretend you are."

"Fuck you. You don't know what it's like if no one cares if you live or die!"

"Maybe they would care if you weren't such a whore who only cared about herself."

"I care, I'd do anything for Luna."

"Is that why you let Gavin and Luna use your house tonight? You're disgusting. You're only trying to turn her into a whore just like you."

"Are you jealous, Attie? Poor Atticus Lodge, always wanting to make the high school's most popular girl fall in love with you. But she'll never see you as more than a faithful dog she can pat on the head and praise sometimes." She reaches out her hand like she's going to touch me, and I step back. "Good dog," she slurs.

"Fuck you, Jules."

"Go chase your own tail, little puppy. Your brother is getting the homecoming queen's cherry tonight and once that's done, you'll cease to exist for her, even as a pet."

"You're a mean drunk, Jules."

"Just leave me alone, Attie. I don't want to play with you tonight. You're not even that good in bed. Your dick is so tiny I barely can feel it inside of me." She snorts and covers her mouth as she hiccups.

I walk away from her. She disgusts me. She's the reason Luna is growing away from me.

It's all her fault. Her and my fucking brother.

CHAPTER FIFTY ONE

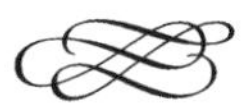

GAVIN

I let us in Jules' house and lock the door behind us. We changed our clothes at a gas station and Luna grabbed a water, but she has barely spoken since. I'm afraid she's changing her mind...

"Alone at last," she says, turning around to smile at me.

"Are you having second thoughts, Moonbeam?"

"No... I'm just..."

"Just what?" I ask her, closing the small distance between us and taking her in my arms, holding her so she can feel me. I need her to know that I'm here, and I'll always be here for her.

"Nervous. I'm so nervous, Gavin and I don't know why."

"We don't have to do this tonight, Luna."

"No! I want to. It's not like that..."

"Then, what is it?

"What if I'm no good at this?"

I look at this woman who apparently has no idea how much I love her. She's grasping her hands so tightly they're white. She looks up at me, her face so scared and earnest that maybe I shouldn't, but I smile.

"Babe," I murmur, shaking my head.

"Gavin, I'm serious—"

"Don't you get it yet, Luna?"

"Get what?"

"Baby, I love you so much. There's nothing about you that could ever disappoint me. Fuck, Luna, I'm over here praying that I can eventually be good enough for you."

"That's crazy," she says shaking her head.

"No, it's not, Luna. Look at you. You're so far above me that I shouldn't have even tried to be in your world."

"I'm glad you did," she responds, softening in my arms.

"Oh yeah? Why's that?"

"Because now you are my world, Gavin." Her words are so sweet, and I can tell from the look in her eyes that she means them. I bend down and pick her up, cradling her against my body. "What are you doing?" Luna laughs, her arms looping behind my neck as I carry her up the stairs.

"Showing you that you're my world too," I tell her, which isn't a lie. But I will admit, it's a tad more romantic than telling her that I'm taking you to bed because I'm dying to be inside of you...

"This isn't Jules' room," she says when we finally get there. I let her slide to the floor then lock the bedroom door. I know Jules said she'd be out all night and most of tomorrow—but it's better to be safe. I don't want anything ruining this night for Luna—for either of us.

"It's a guest room. I wanted... tonight to be special. I was going to get a hotel room..."

"This is better," she says looking up at me. "There are so many roses..."

"I might have gone a little overboard," I mutter, feeling uncomfortable. Still, I move around the room lighting the candles—I might as well make a complete fool of myself. When I'm done, I turn out the overhead light and the room softens with the muted glow from the candles.

"You went to a lot of effort here..."

"Luna, if you're still not ready, you don't have to feel pressured. That's not what this is about."

"I don't feel pressured," she says walking toward me.

"Good, that's the last thing I want. I don't want you to feel like you don't have a choice—"

"Gavin?"

"Yeah, Moonbeam?"

"Shut up and kiss me."

I look at her smiling up at me and like that the nerves disappear. She wants this. She wants me.

Now, I have to make sure she never regrets it.

CHAPTER FIFTY TWO

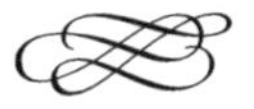

LUNA

"I'm a little nervous, Gavin, but I want this. I want to belong to you."

"We'll belong to each other, Luna. From this moment on, that's just the way it will be. You and me against the world."

"I like that."

I step away from him then, our gazes remaining locked.

"I'm not sure what to do here..."

"What do you want to do, Moonbeam?

"Hide under the covers," I tell him honestly, seeming way too exposed and I'm not even undressed yet.

"Then, do it."

"Really?"

"Tonight is all about what you want, Luna. If you want me to undress you under the covers then I'll do that."

"Have I told you that I love you, Gavin?"

"I've heard it once or twice," he jokes. "Do you want me to blow out the candles?"

"No... I like the candles... it's nice, but still... kind of dark," I tell him, and I know I'm blushing, but I doubt he can see that in this light—something to be thankful for.

"Do you want me to undress under the covers, too?" he asks and my heart melts. I don't know much about being in a relationship—at least one where sex is involved—but, I doubt other guys would be this understanding. That reinforces the fact that I'm doing the right thing giving him my virginity. Gavin is the one and whatever is ahead of us, it will be okay because we will be together.

"It's probably a double standard, but..."

"But?"

"Can I watch you?" I mumble and then I remember what we did the last time we were together and heat fires through my body —along with desire. "Undress I mean. Not what... not what we did before. I mean I liked that—liked it a lot, but I was hoping it would end different this time and I just, I thought—"

"Go get in bed, Luna," Gavin says, smiling at me.

"Oh," I respond, backing away. "I'll just... I'll just get in bed now."

"Good plan, Babe."

Maybe I'm silly, but I love when he calls me babe. My heart feels like it is beating a million miles a minute. I kick off my shoes and socks, feeling all kinds the idiot. Jules told me to pack a sexy nightie and I didn't. It felt weird. I wore a bra and panty set that I liked, they're a soft pink and I think they look good on me, but now that I think about it, Jules was probably right. Gavin probably thinks I'm so lame, that's all I can think as I slide under the cover, still fully clothed in my white shirt and soft blue skirt.

Lame.

"Get that look off your face, Luna," Gavin says, and I jerk my head back to look at him. He has his shirt off already, and my mouth goes dry.

"What look?" I ask, watching as he kicks off his boots. Somehow his socks come off easily and the way he does it, it seems sexy—nothing like how I'm sure I looked. I stare down at his bare feet wondering how he manages to make even them look sexy. Gavin says I'm out of his league, but it's clear that he's out of mine.

"That one that says you're worrying too much," he says, softly, as he pushes his jeans down his body.

Heat moves through my veins at the sight of him standing there in nothing but his boxers. I guess guys aren't supposed to be beautiful, but he so is. I let out a dreamy sigh, because I can't stop myself. Gavin laughs, and I know he heard me. I would probably blush, if my skin wasn't already as red as a tomato. I force myself to drag my eyes back to his face and take in his smile. When his hands move to his boxers, it feels like I'm being hit with a thousand volts of electricity.

I'm not sure I'm ready for this...

"Umm...maybe keep the boxers on for now?" I mumble, my voice sounding as freaked out as I probably look because my nerves are definitely getting the better of me.

He walks unhurriedly to the bed, the same gentle smile on his face, and he gets in the bed with me.

"You've got to quit worrying, Luna. Everything is going to be okay," he murmurs, as I lean up on my elbow to look at him. His hand snakes under my hair to hold the side of my neck and then he kisses me.

I gasp, inhaling and breathing him in as his tongue takes over my mouth, my lungs are filled with the earthy, musky scent of Gavin, and I relax into his kiss.

He's right.

Everything is going to be okay.

Better than okay.

Gavin will make it amazing...

CHAPTER FIFTY THREE

GAVIN

God, there's something about kissing Luna that makes it feel like I'm flying, soaring high above the clouds. Her mouth is so sweet, her moans so tempting and sexy, her actions tentative and heated with desire… she's everything I could dream of and so much more. There's no way to put what she does to me in words.

I just know she owns me.

I kiss her until she's squirming against me, her body moving, pushing into me, wanting more. My breathing is ragged, because I'm as hungry as she seems to be. When our lips break apart, I kiss down the side of her neck, raking my teeth against the soft skin. Her head tilts to give me access, as she whimpers my name. Her fingers bite into my sides, so harshly that it's almost painful—but then, that's a welcome pain. Luna hungry for me? Holding onto me tightly while her eyes are closed, letting me do whatever I want to her?

Definitely welcomed.

"Gavin," she moans when my hand reaches under her shirt to cup her breast.

I squeeze it gently, feeling her nipple pressing against my

palm. My cock is so hard that I'm surprised it doesn't rip through my boxers. I need to hold on until I make sure Luna gets pleasure from this, but I better start moving faster. If I don't, I'll end up coming just like this and that can't happen.

"I'm only going to do what you're comfortable with, Luna."

"Gavin—"

"I mean it. You're the one in control here, Moonbeam." I watch as she fights her nerves and nods her head in agreement. "Can I take your shirt off?'

"I'm such a freak," she mumbles, reaching down to grab her shirt. In the end, we both lift it over her head, and I let it fall to the floor beside the bed.

"You're perfect, Luna. So fucking perfect."

"I'm a mor—"

I kiss her so she'll quit feeling bad. I don't want that. Tonight is only about making her feel good. She gets lost in the kiss and I fight to keep my head, needing to make sure she's completely lost in passion. I undo her bra during the kiss, my movements uncoordinated as I work blindly under the covers.

"Gavin..." Luna whispers as we break apart.

"Close your eyes and just feel, Luna. Just feel."

I kiss down her neck then lower, seeking her breast and latch onto her nipple. I'm rewarded with her moan, her body softening underneath me. My hand moves down her stomach, teasing the soft skin as I flatten my tongue and stroke it against her hard nipple.

"That feels good." Her moan makes me smile almost as much as when I feel her fingers push into my hair and she pulls my head downward against her breast, needing more. I take that as my cue that she's ready.

I slide my hand under her skirt, pushing her panties to the side. I suck hard on her breast, as wet heat meets my fingers. Her pussy is coated with her desire, pooling against the lips, and running along the inside of her thighs. I can feel my hand tremble as I slide my fingers inside of her, not deeply, but teasing her. She opens for me, another signal she wants more and fuck, am I grateful. I'm not sure I can hold on much longer. I work her, sliding my fingers in and out, each time sinking a little deeper—deeper than I ever have before. My thumb pushes against her clit, grinding against it. I can feel her orgasm rising between us—hear it in the heated gasps of air, the way she moans my name and in the restlessness of her body. Her head tosses from side to side, and I feel her body tense right before she falls over the edge, my name on her lips.

It's beautiful and we've only just began...

CHAPTER FIFTY FOUR

GAVIN

I move quickly and the next few minutes are a blur of kissing Luna, pulling off clothes, clumsily putting on a condom and positioning myself over her, my cock pressed against her entrance.

It would have been so easy to push inside of her, taking her virginity before she even came down from her orgasm. Maybe that would have been better, because I know no matter what happens, she's probably going to feel pain—but, that's not what I want.

I've tried to research on ways to make it easier for her—but, the truth is there's not a lot of ways to find things out unless I just start asking around and I wasn't about to do that. Whatever happens between me and Luna will always stay between us.

"Luna."

My voice is hoarse with hunger and the sound comes out almost like a groan. I want to remember this moment for the rest of my life. I want her to remember it.

It's special—Luna is special.

I bend down to kiss her neck, making a path to her ear. Biting on her lobe and sucking it into my mouth, I'm rewarded with her whimper, her body trembling under me as a shudder from her orgasm moves through her.

"Moonbeam, look at me," I beg, pulling back to see if she does as I ask.

Every second seems to take a lifetime. I don't even realize that I'm holding my breath until her beautiful green eyes open to look at me. They're filled with pleasure—pleasure I gave her.

"I love you," she says and the emotion behind those words squeeze my heart. Until Luna, I don't think anyone ever gave a damn about me. Then again, until her, I never really gave a damn about anything.

"I need you to look at me, Luna. I want you to keep your eyes on me the entire time. I want to watch you as I claim your virginity. I want you to watch me as we become one. I don't want either of us to forget anything about this."

If possible, her face softens even more, and I know that my words mean something to her. Luna understands how special she is to me. How special this is—at least I hope she does.

"I'm never going to forget, Gavin," she promises, her voice gentle but full of conviction. Moving her fingers into my hair, she leans up to kiss me, her lips sweet like candy.

I deepen the kiss then pull away to watch her face.

"Now." I mouth the words, I can't be sure I actually voice them because my heartbeat is echoing loudly in my ears. Slowly, I push inside of her, not far, but deep enough that her muscles are clamped down on me, her body tensing at the invasion. "I love you, Luna," I promise, my hand going down to massage her clit. I don't know why. Instinct, I guess. I only know I need to make this good for her.

"Gavin..." she gasps my name and it ends up on a cry, our eyes locked, as I tear through the barrier of her innocence.

"God, Baby," I moan, my heart stuttering in my chest, as I realize that Luna is finally mine.

Completely mine.

I don't move, afraid I'm going to hurt her as I see tears gather in the corner of her eyes. I lean in to kiss them away, taking their salty flavor into me.

"I love you…. I love you… I love you…" I repeat those words with each kiss I place along her neck and down to her breasts. I'm dying to move, but I don't.

I can't.

Not until Luna is ready for me.

Bit by bit her body softens under me and I sink deeper inside, but still I'm afraid to move. Then, I feel Luna's hands slide against my ass.

"More, Gavin, I need more," she pleads like a prayer.

We're so close, almost nose to nose, and I'm lost to the desire I see in her eyes, her breath feathers out against my lips.

"I'll give it to you, Moonbeam. I'll always give it to you," I vow.

Then, I make love to her, using my body, my mouth… my heart and right before I come, I make sure Luna does too.

I don't know if I did everything right, but I know—at least for me—coming inside of Luna, feeling her climax while I'm buried deep inside of her, is beautiful.

And sheer and utter perfection.

CHAPTER FIFTY FIVE

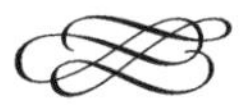

LUNA

"I don't want to leave." I stare at Gavin as I say that. They're simple words, but I feel them all the way to my soul. Last night with Gavin, being able to spend the whole night with him... I never dreamed anything could be that wonderful in all of my life.

"I don't either, Moonbeam," Gavin says, walking to me and wrapping me up in his arms.

I lay my head on his chest and I can hear his heart beating against my ear and it's reassuring. If I had my way, we'd just stay like this.

"I don't know how I'm supposed to be okay with not having you beside me at night now."

"Babe," he says with a smile, his hand under my chin to pull my face up so I'll look at him. Gavin, I'm learning, loves eye contact.

"I'm serious," I grumble. "I don't want you to leave."

"I know, Moonbeam. I feel the same way. But it won't be for long and soon we'll be together all the time."

"When we leave Stone Lake," I tell him, excitement filling me.

"Exactly."

"Where are we going to go?"

"We'll just hop in the truck and drive, Babe. Go wherever the road will take us."

"What if—"

"No worrying. It's just the two of us and together we can tackle it all, Moonbeam."

"You sound so sure, I wish I could be…"

"I will be sure enough for both of us," he promises.

"Have I told you yet today that I love you?"

"I don't think so." He gives me a sly grin.

"*Liar.* I told you in the shower," I remind him.

"Ohhh… yeah the shower. I was distracted at the time."

Heat raises on my face at the heat in his eyes. I was still fighting my nerves this morning when we showered together, but Gavin makes me feel beautiful, and the pleasure we found in each other's arms was definitely worth getting over my bashfulness.

"I noticed." His face clouds for a minute and a chill moves through me that I don't understand.

"We have to be more careful," he says.

"What?" I ask, not understanding.

"I didn't use a condom in the shower, Luna."

"Oh."

"Yeah, oh. I'm so sorry, Moonbeam. I lost my head."

"It's okay, Gavin."

"No, it's not. We have to be more careful. A baby would ruin everything right now."

"Not everything. We'd make it work together," I reassure him, going to wrap my arms around him. He pulls away, looking at me, I can't read the emotion on his face, but I know it is one I don't like.

"It wouldn't work, Luna. Don't you see? If I screwed up and got you pregnant it would mean the end of all of my dreams, of all of our plans."

"I… I don't understand."

"I have to get out of Stone Lake, Luna. It's killing me. Hell, if I stay here much longer, my old man will kill me."

"Gavin—"

"We can't go on the road with a baby. I won't be able to get the training and school I need to be a cop or detective. I need that to be able to give you the kind of home you deserve, the life you deserve. Everything hinges on making sure our plans hold so our dreams will come true, Luna."

"I don't really have any dreams, other than being with you for the rest of my life, Gavin."

"And you will. I just need to be more careful."

"I'm sure it will be fine. You pulled out when you uh… *you know.*"

"Yeah, probably. I'll make sure it doesn't happen again. To be sure, we need to get you on birth control as soon as possible," he says, softening some and taking me back in his arms.

"I can't do that. Not here in Stone Lake at least, it would get back to my mom. You know how this place is."

"Then, it will be the first thing we do when we leave here. Until then, we'll just use condoms."

"Okay," I tell him, feeling uncomfortable talking about this. Something about the way he talks about it and the near panic I saw on his face when he realized he wasn't wearing a condom, makes me feel weird. I mean, I don't want to have a baby either. Gavin's right, that would be the last thing we need to happen. But, still, his reaction and words hurt my feelings. I'd be lying if I didn't admit that—at least to myself. "I thought Jules would be back by now," I tell him, needing to change the subject so that he will quit worrying.

"I did too. I need to get going, I have work today, but I'm not leaving you here alone."

"She was pretty hammered last night. I can call my mom to come and get me. I don't want to make you late for work."

"How about I take you home?"

"I don't think—"

"Just like a block from your house. You can tell your mom you hitched a ride there. I'd just feel better knowing you're not here alone. I'm not sure there's anything to the notes that Jules has been getting, but it's better to be safe."

"Okay, if you're sure."

"I'm positive."

"Then, I guess we better head out," I respond with a sigh, hating that I can't stay with Gavin longer.

"Tomorrow is Monday, Babe. I'll be with you at school."

"Yeah, but I'm still going to miss you."

"I'll miss you too, Moonbeam, more than you know." He takes my hand and I follow him out the door as he locks up. Being without him is not going to be easy, but it's not too much longer until graduation and then we can be together all the time.

CHAPTER FIFTY SIX

GAVIN

"Well, don't you two look sickeningly happy," Atticus sneers.

I tighten up, despite the joy of having Luna back in my arms. I know my brother is only trying to get to me. I should ignore him, but it's hard.

"We are," Luna says, looking up at me with a wink. Despite having Atticus so close, I smile, bend down and kiss her. We're outside. It's warm out for a change and I'm on the ground leaning against the trunk of a tree, Luna lying down, her head in my lap, our hands linked lazily against her stomach.

"Do you want something, Atticus?" I ask him, irritation laced in my voice. I won't get a lot of time with Luna, and I'd rather not have to share any of it with my fuck-head brother.

Atticus ignores me, which is not surprising. I twirl Luna's hair around my finger, biding my time until the asshole leaves.

"Have you seen Jules, Luna?"

"I haven't. She didn't come to school today. I got a text from her last night that said she was sick, and she'd check in with me later. I figured she was still hung over."

"Probably. She was pretty drunk Saturday night. I just wanted to check on her."

"I'll tell her to shoot you a message tonight when I talk to her, Attie."

"Sounds good. I'll catch you later, Luna."

"You don't have to leave, Attie."

"Let him go," I tell her, my gaze locked on Atticus's. I see the hate that flashes over his facial features, but I don't really give a fuck. He was bragging last night about the fact he watched Dad beat me. He left me, not knowing—or caring—if I lived or died. Considering Dad came after me because I defended Atticus, that pretty much did me in. I don't care what happens to the asshole now.

"Gavin, don't," Luna says, sitting up.

"Don't worry about it, Luna. I'm used to Gavin treating me like shit. He may be nicer to you, but eventually you'll see the real him," Atticus says, turning away.

"That's rich coming from you," I growl and since Luna is no longer in my lap, I stand up.

"What's that mean?"

"Don't you ever get tired of the damn games, Atticus? Doesn't it exhaust you to act like the good guy around Luna when both of us know you're nothing but a piece of shit?"

"I'll tell you what I get tired of, Gavin. I get tired of you acting like you're so much better than me. You're not. You're nothing. One day Luna will realize that and then where will you be? *Alone.* Probably lost in a bottle just like our father. You're already halfway there." He snickers, but I don't find anything he just said funny.

"How in the fuck do you figure that?"

"Sniffing around Luna, knowing she's too good for you. You only want her because she has money. What's next, brother? Are you going to knock Luna up? Isn't that how Dad got Mom? Are you going to pretend to save the day and then leave her miserable too, until one day she just has enough and leaves you behind?"

"You forget they had you too."

"I didn't forget. I'll never forget. I know exactly who I am. You're the one who doesn't know."

"Know what?"

"That you're scum."

"That's rich coming from you, brother."

"We're not brothers, we might have the same mother, but that's it. You're the reason for all of the shit in my life," Atticus boasts.

"Bullshit," I laugh. "I don't know what you've convinced yourself of, but it's not true."

"It is. That's what *my* father told me the night we were fighting. He told me that he used to be a good man, used to have plans, but then he met a woman who he wanted, only she didn't want him back."

"Shut up," I growl, wondering how he could have made up these stories in his head and believe them.

"He wasn't good enough for her, until some drifter left her knocked up and she needed him to step in and keep her respectable. So, you see, Gavin? You're the reason Dad drinks himself into a stupor. You're a constant reminder that our father married a whore," Atticus sneers before he stomps off.

I'm left standing there, not sure what I'm feeling. I thought nothing could surprise me anymore, I was wrong.

I'm definitely surprised.... I just don't know how I really feel about Atticus's revelation.

"Gavin? Are you okay?" Luna asks softly.

"I don't know," I tell her honestly, rubbing the back of my neck.

"I'm going to sign myself out and go hunt down my father, Luna."

"Gavin, maybe you should—"

"I'll be fine," I tell her kissing her quickly. "I'll call you tonight."

"Okay…" she says. I can hear the worry in her voice, and I don't want to concern her, but I'm not sure what I'm experiencing right now. I don't know how to explain that to her and I don't know what to do. The thought of Atticus not being my brother doesn't bother me. I think it's pretty clear that there's no love lost between us. Still, the revelation has sent me for a loop. There's a part deep inside of me praying it's true. Either way I have to know.

I have to.

CHAPTER FIFTY SEVEN

LUNA

"Gavin, something is wrong, I know it."

"Babe—"

"She won't answer her phone. It's been three days and she's texted me twice to tell me that she's okay but checking out for a bit. *What does that even mean?*"

"Babe, maybe it means just what she said. You know yourself that she hasn't been happy for a while. Maybe she went out of town with her parents."

"She hates her parents and they go out of town for swinger parties. Jules would die before going anywhere with them."

"Swinger parties?"

"Exactly."

"There's a mental image I didn't need," he says, wincing. I don't blame him, I don't like to think about it either.

"I'm really worried about her, Gavin."

"Did you call her parents? You have their number, right?"

"Yeah, they said they've been in touch with Jules and she's fine."

"There, if she's talking to her parents—"

"She's texted them, like she has with me. That's it. Don't you think that's strange? As much as Jules loves to talk that she's cut herself off from everyone?"

"Okay, so what do we do?" Gavin asks, frowning down at me. I look around the hallway, desperate. I keep praying that Jules will walk through the doors and come in yelling and laughing at me for being so scared. I've been wanting that for three days. It hasn't happened and she doesn't magically appear now either. Out of the corner of my eye I see Darren. I start walking toward him.

"Luna—"

I hear Gavin call my name, but I keep walking. Darren jerks his head up to look at me as I reach him. He looks guilty and he should. Meghan Flint is pressed up against him tightly.

"Have you heard from Jules?"

"No, why should I?"

"Because the two of you are dating?" I question, my voice full of sarcasm as I give Meghan a dirty look.

"We're not. We broke up at prom. I haven't talked to her since."

"You broke up with her?"

"She was drunk off her ass and accusing me of cheating on her. I don't need that kind of drama."

"Drama. Right. I guess she was imagining the way you were hanging all over Meghan then. Oh wait, but here Meghan is, right?"

"So? It's not like her and Darren were married," Meghan whines. "Not that it's any business of yours Marshall, why don't you step back?"

"You haven't heard anything from her since prom?" I ask, ignoring Meghan, even though I'd like to take my frustration out on her.

"Why would I?"

"Shit," I mumble turning back around to look at Gavin. "I'm telling you something is wrong, Gavin," I tell him, my voice trembling. He takes me in his arms, his hands combing through my hair reassuringly.

"It's going to be okay, Moonbeam. We'll find her," he says, and I want to believe him...

I just don't think I can.

"I'm sorry. I shouldn't be laying all this on you. I know you're upset right now yourself," I utter as he pulls me back down the hall and away from Darren. We haven't really talked about the things Atticus laid on him Monday, but I know it's still bothering him. He's been really quiet and sometimes when we're talking, it feels like he is a hundred miles away.

"I'm fine, just got a lot on my mind right now," he confesses.

"I wish you would talk to me about it. Maybe I can help," I offer.

"Gavin, son, I need you to come with me," the principal says, coming up behind us and surprising me.

There's something in his tone that worries me. I study him noticing there are three deputies standing behind him. My hold on Gavin tightens. Something is going on here and whatever it is, it is not good.

"What's up," Gavin asks, he might sound relaxed, but his body is tense against me.

"You need to come with me," the principal says again. All around us people are gathering, knowing something is up. I ignore them and instead focus on what is in front of me.

"Tell me what's going on here," Gavin argues and that's when the deputies move up beside the principal.

"You're Gavin Lodge?" one of them asks.

"Yeah," Gavin answers, confused.

"We're going to have to ask you to come down to the station with us."

"What's going on here?" Atticus asks, appearing behind us. Gavin ignores him, and I don't have time to look at him. My heart is beating crazily in my chest and my palms are damp with sweat. I keep holding on tightly to Gavin, afraid to let him go.

"Come with us son, it will go easier that way."

"What will go easier? What in the hell is happening? I'm not going anywhere until you tell me what's going on," Gavin growls, anger bleeding through his words.

"We'll explain it down at the station," the deputy says.

"You'll explain it now. I've got the right to know what's going on."

"We were hoping to do this privately, but you're not leaving us any choice."

"Any choice on what? I don't understand—"

"Gavin Lodge, you're under arrest," the deputy announces, jerking Gavin from my arms, and twisting his hands behind his back. Gavin lets him, his head twisting to find me, his face looking bleak.

Oh God, this can't be happening...

"What am I under arrest for? You could at least tell me that!" Gavin growls.

"You're under arrest for the murder of Julie Sampson," the deputy responds.

My heart feels like it stops mid-beat. My body flushes, but with a cold heat that seems to chill me all the way to the bone.

Jules.... Dead...

I hear screaming, and I barely register the sound is coming from me. My legs give out and I'm dropping to the floor. I feel arms go around me, but I ignore them.

Jules... Dead...

I can't breathe. I can't breathe. *I. Can't. Breathe.*

"Luna, I didn't do this," Gavin yells over his shoulder looking at me. I can barely make him out through the tears in my eyes as sobs wrack through my body. "I didn't do this," he yells again, and then he's lost to someone screaming in pain...

And this time I don't even realize it's coming from me.

CHAPTER FIFTY EIGHT

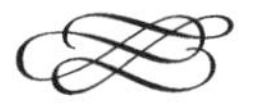

GAVIN

"Hello."

"Luna," I breathe. "Thank God."

"Gavin?"

"Are you okay, Moonbeam?" I ask, breathing into the phone.

I lean my head against the wall, close my eyes and try to picture her. I've been worried since the moment they brought me in. All I could see was the way she crumbled before my eyes and I was helpless, because I couldn't get to her and comfort her.

"Gavin," she breathes. "They let you go? Oh God, I was so worried, and my dad showed up. He wouldn't let me follow you and—"

"They didn't let me go, Luna. I'm still here."

"Then how are you—"

"They gave me one phone call, I called the only person that matters."

"Gavin, no. You need to call your Dad. You need him to—"

"He's not my Dad, Moonbeam. He's nothing to me," I tell her. What I'm not telling her is that I really had no one here in Stone Lake to call. As for dear old *dad.* He's been here, helping them create a case against me. He even did it sober. I'm not sure I've seen him sober in years, but he was when they escorted him by me to take his statement.

He even did it smiling.

"We have to find someone to help you," she whispers so quietly into the phone that it's hard to make out what she's saying.

"I'm not important, Moonbeam. I just need to make sure you're okay."

"Jules is dead, Gavin." It's a simple statement, but tears and pain ooze through it and I hold the phone away from my mouth as I curse the fact that I can't be there with her. I should be there.

She needs me.

"I know, Baby," I tell her, wishing I could hold her.

"They… They found her with a rose, like the last girl."

Fuck.

"I'm sorry, Luna."

"Once they figure out that there's no way you committed the murder, they'll let you go, right? They have to know that the guy who killed the other girls did this one too."

"I gotta go, Moonbeam. They only let me talk for a few minutes. I just… I wanted to know you're okay."

"Gavin? They're going to let you go, right? They can't keep you, not now that they know she's been killed by the same killer."

"I don't know what's going to happen, Babe. All I know is that I need you to believe in me. I need you to know that I didn't do this."

"I know that, Gavin. You don't even have to ask me that."

I close my eyes. I've seen the looks I got when I was led into the police station. I saw the looks I got from the students as I was escorted out. Hell, I saw the looks the principal gave me, and his secretary. I saw them all. There's not one person in this town that believes I'm innocent…

"Promise me, Babe. Promise me you believe me."

"I believe you, Gavin. You didn't do this."

"Times up, Lodge," the deputy says from his corner, his face cold.

"I gotta go, Luna."

"Gavin, no. Don't go. Tell me what I can do to help. Tell me—"

"I'll be okay. I love you, Moonbeam."

I hang up and that poison in the pit of my stomach churns. I've been through a lot of shit in my lifetime. You'd think I could handle anything, but right now I feel fear. I have from the first moment they brought me in.

They won't even tell me why they suspect me, they keep asking me the same questions over and over. I've got a bad feeling it doesn't matter what I answer. Their mind is made up and all the people they've talked to is only helping them.

I close my eyes and immediately a picture of Roy Lodge's cold smile flashes in my mind.

I'm fucked...

CHAPTER FIFTY NINE

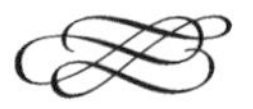

LUNA

This could go bad.

Really bad.

I'm desperate though. There's nothing else I can do. Gavin has been locked up for three weeks. He had a damn arraignment and Atticus said they set his bond at one-hundred thousand dollars. They say that is low when compared to what he was charged with, but that doesn't matter. It might as well have been a hundred dollars. Gavin doesn't have that kind of money and there's no way his father is going to help him. Roy Lodge is the star witness for the prosecution. Gavin's picture has been in every newspaper in Maine. His face on the news—even the national news. I've begged my parents to help and that wasn't easy. Talking to my dad and asking him for anything right now was hard, but he won't listen. They've been keeping me locked up too. I can't leave the house. Mom or Dad take me to school and pick me up. It appears they can hate each other, but the one thing they can agree on is holding me hostage.

It doesn't just end with them either. I'm a prisoner at school, too. The principal seems to constantly follow me around while

I'm there. If he doesn't, then the vice-principal or his secretary does. There hasn't been one chance to sneak away.

Not one.

I might as well be locked up with Gavin at this point and considering I stole my mother's car while she was in the shower, I probably will be. I had to though. This is the first chance I've had. Usually her and Dad tag team, so one or the other watches me constantly and if it's only one of them, they literally lock my door. Dad had the locks changed so it locked from the outside.

It's ridiculous.

Today, though, Mom slipped up. I played hooky from school and because she felt bad that I was sick, when she took her morning shower, she left my door unlocked in case I needed to run to the bathroom in the hall. The minute I heard the shower turn on, I bolted. I had spied Mom's keys lying on the counter, when I came down under the guise of getting some ginger ale for my stomach. Lady luck continued to be on my side when they were still there. I grabbed them, then sprinted to the garage.

I'm sure Mom has discovered the clump under the covers of my bed is not me by now. She may have even discovered that her car is gone. I figure the worst she can do is call the police and since I'm headed there, I don't really care.

At this point, I'm so mad at my parents that I don't care what they think or how they react to anything. I've been screaming at them for weeks that Gavin is innocent. I told them there was no way he could have killed Jules. They either think I'm lying, or they don't care.

I'm starting to believe it's a combination of both.

Still, I know I can save Gavin and since no one else is even trying to, I have to do this.

I park the car on the street, my hands tightening on the steering wheel so hard that my fingers go white from the pressure. I'm a nervous wreck.

What if they don't believe me? What if they don't even bother to check my story?

I hold my head down against the wheel and calm my churning stomach. I wasn't exactly lying to Mom. I've been sick for two days. I can't keep anything down. I know it's stress. Stress and pain. If Mom and I were talking, maybe I would have handled all of this differently. Only we're not talking. I feel like she's let me down too. She didn't even let me go to Jules' memorial service.

I should have been there...

I climb out of the car and walk toward the station on shaky legs. I feel like there are a million eyes on me, but I don't look around to actually see if there are. I open the door to the police station and walk to the front desk. I look around the room and see several cops that I've seen in town all sitting at desks. I swallow down the bile that rises when I see some men in suits standing talking to the sheriff. One has a jacket on, and the jacket says FBI on it. Atticus said that he was told they were coming in and were going to take control. Are they here for Gavin now?

Probably.

That's another reason I'm so desperate.

"Can I help you?"

I look at the man at the front desk. Stone Lake is a small town, but I don't know him. I can't even place him. I don't know why that's important right now, and I don't guess it is. I just... I thought maybe if I knew someone here, it would help...

I wring my hands together, my stomach churning. I pray I don't get sick. Considering the last two days that's entirely possible and somehow, I don't think throwing up on the cops will help either Gavin or me.

"I'm here to give a statement."

"A statement?"

"Yes."

"What are you wanting to give a statement about?"

"I'm Luna Marshall, Gavin Lodge's girlfriend, and I'm here to give a statement on his behalf."

"I'm afraid that doesn't matter right now. You'll have to talk to his public defender. This is out of our hands," he says, his face going hard.

Panic hits me again.

Doesn't matter? Talk to his public defender?

If I don't give this statement now, I'll never get the chance. My parents will lock me up so tight that I'll never see daylight again.

I have to do this now.

I notice out of the corner of my eye that the men in suits and the FBI-coat-guy are looking at me. I have their attention.

Oh God.

"You have to listen to me," I say, speaking louder, hoping they hear me... hoping anyone will listen to me. "I need to talk to you about Gavin Lodge."

"Lady, I don't know what—"

"I can prove he's innocent. I can prove that you've arrested and charged the wrong person in Jules..." I get choked up when I say her name. A familiar pain lances through me, but I push through. "In the murder of Julie Sampson," I finally finish.

"You have proof?"

The question comes from the guy in the jacket. I look up at him and I don't know why, but I get the feeling that he wants me to have proof. He looks almost... *friendly.*

"I do," I tell him. "He couldn't have murdered Jules, because... he was with me."

"You can prove that?"

"Yeah."

He puts his hand on my back and looks at the sheriff. "I'll be conducting this interview. You're welcome to join, or not. I don't really give a damn," he says, and I can tell the sheriff isn't happy. There's some major friction there. Suddenly, I'm even more glad the guy in the coat is here.

Maybe he will help.

CHAPTER SIXTY

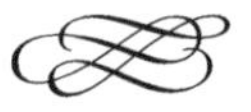

GAVIN

"Good news, Gavin."

I look up as Detective Dern comes through the door. I'm leaning against the cell wall, sitting on my mattress, which is so paper thin that I can feel the steel underneath it. I like Detective Dern. He's been decent to me from the beginning, I get the impression he believes me. He thinks I didn't kill Jules or any of the other women. The problem is I don't have any proof, that coupled with the fact that the people who they deem as my "family" have all testified against me...

I'm fucked.

"I doubt it," I tell him, staring at the wall, refusing to let hope rise. I gave up hope a couple weeks back. I haven't heard from Luna. She didn't even come to my arraignment. She said she believed in me, but apparently that has changed. I'm truly alone. I rake my hand through my hair, pulling my head down to my knees. The smell of the orange jumpsuit they had me put on smells musty. It's the same smell that haunts me in this cell. I know Detective Dern is trying to help me, he doesn't want me to give up hope, but it's too late.

Maybe it always has been.

"Chin up, Lodge. Things are about to get a whole lot better for you."

"Is the guard going to be cuter when he does the body search on me this time?" I joke, though there's no humor in my voice.

There's actually nothing in my voice, because there's nothing in me.

I'm empty.

Detective Dern opens my cell door.

Is he going to give me another one of his heart to heart talks? I don't think I can handle that right now.

"You're free, boy."

"Yeah, right."

"I'm serious. Right now, as we speak, all charges against you are being dropped. I even saw to it myself that the prosecutor compiled the proper papers and hand delivered them to the judge."

"I... you're... You mean it?"

"Yep. Most days my job sucks, this is a win for the good guys. You're free, Gavin."

"How?" I ask, still afraid to believe it.

"Luna Marshall."

"Luna? Do you know Luna?"

"I met her a week ago. She's a brave young woman."

"Luna was here? I don't understand. How could she get the charges dismissed?"

"She signed a statement and gave private testimony to the judge that you were with her the night of the murder."

"How is that different than what I've been telling everyone?"

"You never gave a name, son. I asked you to, and you refused."

"Luna didn't need to be drawn into this mess. I had people who had to agree that I was at the prom, though."

"Yeah, but so was Jules. Luna's testimony was different."

"Why's that?"

"She gave details, that included places you stopped when you left the prom. It took us a week to check out her story, but we did it. Once the judge saw videotape of you at the gas station and later on the security camera of a local dairy bar, showing you were clearly with Luna at the time of the murder..."

Detective Dern shrugs his shoulders, leaving me to draw my own conclusion.

"Where's Luna at now?"

"Right now? I'd assume at school or locked up at her parents' home. I don't think Mr. and Mrs. Marshall are big fans of yours, son."

"Do you blame them?"

"They're just trying to protect their daughter. I have a suspicion that if I had a daughter, I'd be the same way."

"You don't have kids?"

"Don't even have a wife. Tried once, but she said I was more married to the job and not to her. I reckon she was right. It's hard to have a family in this line of work, son. That might be something you want to think about, if you're serious about applying for the Bureau someday."

"That dreams gone," I mumble, still trying to wrap my head around the fact that I'm free and that this nightmare is over.

"Bullshit. If you want it and work hard, it can be yours, Gavin."

I hold my head down. I've had this talk with Dern. He's spent a lot of time checking on me. I told him my dream of being a detective one day in weakness. Now I'm embarrassed that he knows.

"I checked out all those papers you gave me. My record's not going to be clear anymore and how in the hell am I going to go to college and support myself... too?" I started to add Luna's name to that, but now I don't know where she stands with things. For all I know, she never wants to see me again.

"You can take out loans, get grants. There's help out there, but more than that. You can stay with me while you're in school."

"Yeah, right."

"I'm being straight with you, Gavin. If you're serious about entering this field I'm willing to help you."

"Why would you do that? Why would you do any of this?"

"Let's just say I see something in you that reminds me of myself."

"I don't know what to say…" I tell him. There's hope inside of me, I thought it had died but now I can feel it coming back to life, spreading through my system.

Light where once was nothing but darkness.

"I'll make sure your record isn't a problem even after the charges are dropped, sometimes an arrest history and you've had the fight at school and now this, can cause issues. I'll smooth those over. In exchange you keep your head down and work hard."

It'd be stupid to cry in front of him right now, but I have the urge to do it. He hands me a piece of paper, I grab it and look down at the phone numbers that are written on it.

"What's this?"

"You get back to school. You graduate. Once that's done, Gavin, you call me."

"I… I don't know how to thank you, Mr. Dern."

"Call me Lawrence and you can thank me by studying and working your ass off."

"I will. I promise. You won't be disappointed in me. I can't wait to tell Luna."

"About that…"

"Luna? What's wrong?" I ask him a spike of fear piercing through the goodness that had begun to take hold.

"Her parents are threatening to prosecute you for statutory rape if you continue to try and see their daughter."

"They can't do that!"

"I'm afraid they can, son."

"But Luna's eighteen."

"She is now, but she wasn't when you two first started your relationship."

"But we didn't. I mean she… we didn't…"

He puts his hand on my shoulder, to try and calm me, but it doesn't help.

The idea of being thrown back in jail, now that I'm finally free. The threat of losing my freedom again, having to go through more body searches, being arrested and handcuffed and dragged into court…. I've never had one, but if I were going to have a panic attack, it would be now.

"She told them that, but it doesn't matter. They have witnesses willing to testify that you took advantage of Luna when she was sixteen and that she's been coerced into giving you an alibi and into continuing a relationship."

"That's bullshit. Who would—"

"Your own father and brother and a few other classmates at school."

"What the fuck," I growl, standing up. I slam my fist into the block wall. Pain slices through my body, but I don't care.

"Listen, I know it sucks now and you think this girl is the one—"

"She *is* the one," I argue, yelling it out, because it's true.

"I won't argue she's not a good girl and it's clear she loves you, but, Gavin, you need to think with your head here."

"What I need to do is get Luna and leave fucking Stone Lake as far behind as I can."

"Then load up your crap and head out of town with me. I'll be leaving at the end of the week. You can finish your diploma through summer school. I can arrange that for you."

"I'm not leaving without Luna."

"Son, I can fix your record this time. I'll be honest, I don't think anything would come of the charges her parents would press, but it would lead to an arrest and your record will be blotted with that shit. I can't fix that. There's also a chance that this small town will sew you up because they can. A lot of them are blaming you for the death of the Sampson girl, despite us letting you go. Your face, like it or not, has been made famous with this shit."

That fear and panic is back, so heavy that it makes it hard to breathe. I study Dern's face and I don't doubt that he's telling me the truth. I have a choice to make, but there's no real choice. I need Luna to breathe, but can I risk the fact that having her may destroy me?

Without Luna I was never really much to begin with...

"I can't leave Luna behind, Mr. Dern."

He frowns at me and I can see the disappointment on his face. He reaches out his hand to me. "If you change your mind, you have my number."

I nod, my throat too clogged with panic and other emotions to form a reply. I shake his hand and follow him out of my cell.

I have only one plan.

I'm going to load my truck up and grab Luna and get the fuck out of Stone Lake forever.

I hope doing that doesn't get me locked back up in jail...

CHAPTER SIXTY ONE

LUNA

"Well?" Attie asks from behind my locker door.

I scream. I can't help it. My nerves are on end and I feel like I'm dying inside. "Attie, you shouldn't sneak up on me like that."

"Sorry, I've just been worrying about you. Did you find out yet?"

I frown. I don't want to tell him. I need to tell Gavin first, but Atticus is all I have right now. If it wasn't for him, I wouldn't even know for sure....

"Thanks for buying...*that* for me."

"What did it say?"

"It's the first test I've passed in weeks," I tell him, refusing to look him in the eye. I'm too lost in my head. I'm scared—terrified and I haven't seen Gavin in what feels like forever. I need him... *desperately.*

"Luna, does that mean..."

"Keep your voice down," I growl. "I'm pregnant."

"Fuck."

"That was my reaction. Oh, Attie, what am I going to do?"

"There's a clinic—"

"No!"

"Luna, it would be the best thing for—"

"I'm not getting rid of my baby, Attie. It's not happening."

"Okay, fine. So, what are you going to do?"

"Have you seen Gavin? Can you get a message to him for me?"

"He came home last night and packed up his crap. I don't know where he's at."

"Shit."

I really don't want to cry, but I can feel the tears gather in the corners of my eyes. It just all seems so hopeless. I don't know what to say to Gavin. He made it clear he didn't want a baby, and I can't say that I blame him. How will he react when he finds out that I'm pregnant? Will he be mad at me?

Will he hate me?

I know it involved both of us, but most girls my age are on birth control, or at least have an idea of what they're getting involved in when they have sex. I should have reminded him to put the condom on. I should…

"Luna? Can I talk to you?" I look up to see Wally standing there.

"Luna's busy right now," Attie says, but I ignore him. He's trying to be protective right now, but Wally is a good guy—plus he's one of Gavin's only friends. Maybe he can tell me something about Gavin…

Anything.

"What's up, Wally?"

"Can we talk for a minute? Privately?"

"Luna doesn't want to—"

"I'm fine, Attie. Can you give Wally and me a little privacy?" I ask him. His eyes narrow and I know he's not happy. He nods his head stiffly and stomps off, clearly upset.

"Sorry about that. Attie has become protective of me after everything that has happened."

"He's something alright. You do know that he's one of the main ones that testified against Gavin, right?"

"He didn't really have a choice, Wally. His father threatened him. I don't know how much you and Gavin have talked about Mr. Lodge, but—"

"We've talked enough, but I am just warning you, Luna. Don't trust Atticus."

"Why?"

"Ask Gavin."

"That will be kind of hard, since I don't know when I'll see him again."

"He's at school today."

"He is?!?! Where? I haven't seen him. Can you take me—"

"The principal is keeping him out of the classrooms. He's been doing his work in the office. I got to see him at lunch. He wanted me to get a message to you."

"What message?"

"He asked if you could meet him out by the concession building on the football field during the awards ceremony Saturday night? I told him the only place your parents have allowed you to go is to the senior events and that they're always close by."

"I… yeah. I'll be there. It will take me a bit to get away from my mom. The ceremony starts at seven. Can you tell him I'll be waiting for him around seven thirty?"

"Yeah. Do yourself a favor and don't tell Atticus that, Luna."

"You really don't trust him."

"And you shouldn't either."

"I won't tell him," I promise, wondering what Atticus has done that has set Wally so against him. I know Gavin has issues with him, but maybe it's deeper than I realized.

"Good. Later, Luna."

"See ya, Wally," I tell him, but it doesn't matter, Wally is already walking away.

CHAPTER SIXTY TWO

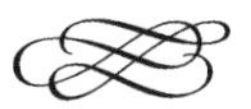

LUNA

"Hello, Miss Marshall." My head jerks up when I hear that voice. I know it.

"Agent Dern? What are you doing here? Is something wrong with Gavin?"

"Not exactly. I was wondering if we might talk a moment."

"What do you mean, not exactly?"

"Gavin is fine, at least for now."

"Oh…" I respond, his comment kind of weird. "My father is waiting for me. If I don't get to the car—"

"I have his permission to speak with you. Will you sit down with me in the cafeteria for a minute?"

"I… I guess… Where is Gavin?"

"He and his friend Wally left a few minutes ago. I waited until he was gone to seek you out."

"Why?" I ask.

He doesn't answer at first. Instead he leads me from the hallway into the lunchroom. It's eerily quiet and completely empty. Agent Dern grabs the first table we pass and pulls out a seat for me. I sit down, frowning as he does the same.

"You're meeting with Gavin Saturday night," he says, surprising me.

"How do you know that?" I kind of evade.

"Gavin told me."

"Oh," I respond breathing easier. "You've spoken to Gavin. Is he okay? Does he know that I still believe him? I haven't been able to talk to him at all. I'm worried. The last time I spoke to him he—"

"He's fine, Luna. Can I call you Luna?"

"Yeah…"

"He's fine. He has a very big decision in front of him."

"He does?" I whisper, my hand going to my stomach. Agent Dern can't see that, it's hidden by the table itself, but what if he knows.

Surely that can't be what he's talking about.

"I've offered Gavin a place to stay and to help make sure he gets through school. He wants to work in law enforcement, and I'd like to see that happen. I see a lot of potential in Gavin."

"Oh my God! Gavin will be so excited. That's all he's ever wanted," I almost squeal. I grab Agent Dern's arm and hold onto it in my excitement. "He has to be so happy. I can't believe this. Thank you, Agent Dern. Thank you so much."

"He turned me down, Luna."

"What? No way. Gavin wouldn't do that. This is his dream. You must have misunderstood."

"He turned me down because of you."

"Me? I don't understand. I won't stand in Gavin's way. I want him to have his dream."

"But he won't leave Stone Lake without you, Luna."

"Oh… and you don't want me to be with him. I mean, I get it. That's okay. Gavin and I can still see each other and once he's out of school we can—"

"It's not so much that as the fact that if he tries to take you with him, or pursue any kind of relationship with you, your parents will prosecute him. You were there the day your father warned me of that."

"Well, yeah. But I'm eighteen and—"

"There have been witnesses that say you were only sixteen when the relationship began and was consummated."

"But... that's crazy," I accuse.

"Maybe, but they've all signed affidavits."

"Who?"

"That's not important, I just—"

"Who?" I growl, my hand clutching tightly against my stomach.

"Gavin's father—"

"He's just a jerk."

"Jules' Mom and Dad."

"Come on, they're not even in town most of the time!" I snap.

"Gavin's brother."

"Atticus?" I ask, remembering Wally's warning now.

"And a couple of classmates. A Larry Reynolds and a Darren—"

"Just stop," I murmur, sick to my stomach.

I'm going to throw up. I've been doing it all the time lately. I've lost fifteen pounds because I haven't been able to eat. That's what made me check to see if I was pregnant. I swallow the bile back down, hoping I can get control of it in time. I don't want Agent Dern thinking I'm weak or realizing I'm pregnant. I need to be the one to tell Gavin.

"You see the problem."

"Not really. They can't prosecute him on that, surely. Not when I'm eighteen and willing to testify to the truth."

"They might not, then again, maybe they will. Either way it doesn't matter. Another arrest on Gavin's permanent record will pretty much ensure that the FBI will pass him over."

"Pass him over?"

"By choosing you, Luna, Gavin is giving up his dream. He's

giving up his one chance for a future—a good future. I don't want to see that happen."

"What do you want me to do?" I ask him, but I know. I know and suddenly I hate Agent Dern. I hate him more than anyone I've ever met.

"I want you to let Gavin go, Miss Marshall." His words are softly spoken, and I can see the pity in his eyes.

His words destroy me.

CHAPTER SIXTY THREE

GAVIN

"Luna." I grab her, pulling her behind the building, before she even finishes walking to me. I take her into my arms, pressing her against me, burying my head in her neck and breathing in her scent.

"Gavin—"

"Fuck, Moonbeam, you feel so good in my arms. I was scared I'd never have that again."

"Gavin," she sobs, her body shaking, but finally she softens against me, her hands going around me to hold onto me tightly.

Finally.

"I've missed you so damn much."

"I've missed you too," she replies, her voice muffled because her mouth is against my shoulder. I move a hand to her neck, holding her gently, tilting her head up, and capturing her mouth in mine. It feels like a million years since I've kissed her.

Once we pull away, I stand back, keeping my hand on her neck and look at her.

Really look at her.

"You've lost weight."

"It's been a rough month."

"God. Has it been a month since we've seen each other, Moonbeam?"

"Longer," she murmurs.

"Are you okay?"

"I'm fine. How about you? I know it had to be horrible there. I wanted to see you, but they wouldn't let me."

"It was hell. I was in county lock up for a while. Once Lawrence got there, he had them bring me back up to the Sheriff's office. That was better."

"Lawrence?"

"Agent Dern. He said he met you."

"Yeah, we've met," she says. Her face goes pale and I feel her tremble in my hold.

"Are you okay?"

"I... I've not been feeling well."

"You're sick?"

"It's nothing. Probably a stomach virus or something."

"Luna, I want to leave right after graduation. We need to plan, especially since we don't get to see each other."

"Gavin—"

"You can start sneaking things you want to take with you to school and Wally will get them to me."

"Gavin, I don't.... it's not going to work."

"It's not ideal, Moonbeam, but it will be okay. We have a little time before graduation. How long do you think you have before your Mom comes looking for you?"

"Not long," she says, her head going down to look at the ground.

"Hey, look at me," I urge her, tilting her head up to look at me. It guts me when I see the tears in her eyes. "Don't cry, Babe. It will work out. I'll take care of you, I promise."

"What happens if we leave and my parents go after you?"

"How can they?"

"They have witnesses lined up against you, Gavin. They are saying that I—"

"I know, Agent Dern told me," I inform her, stopping her from talking. I don't even want to hear her say that shit. I step back, rubbing the back of my neck, wondering how to reassure her, when I'm worried myself. "It doesn't matter, Luna. We'll be far away from Stone Lake, living our lives. No judge is going to listen to that bullshit."

"But what happens if they arrest you, Gavin? You know my father won't give up. He won't."

"Then, we'll weather it until the judge hears the whole story. You're mine, Luna. I love you. We belong to each other. We can face all of it, Moonbeam. We just have to face it together."

"Gavin—"

I see the sadness, the pain in her face and I see the bleakness in her eyes, where once I saw happiness and hope. Desperation fills me. I feel Luna slipping away and I don't know if I can live if that happens. She's rooted so deep inside of me that I think if you cut me, she'd be in my blood. She's the best part of me.

"Don't you love me anymore, Luna? Are you done with me?" I question her, and I can't keep the pain out of my voice. I don't even try to. I let her see it.

"Of course I do. Gavin, I love you so much. I'm just trying to protect you," she cries, tears streaming down her face. "I only want to protect you," she adds, the words coming out like a moan that are torn from her.

I pull her back into my arms, our gazes locked, tears coming from both of us, her body shaking from her tears, mine from the sheer effort of breathing.

"Then, don't leave me, Luna. If you did... I don't think I'd survive. You're my reason to keep going, Moonbeam. You're all that's keeping me sane."

I'm begging. I know it. For Luna, I'd get on my knees and beg without shame.

I stand there looking at her, holding her and knowing my entire life hinges on this moment. Her eyes close and her head goes down, her body softening, and a small spark of hope comes to life.

She's going to choose me… *Choose to fight with me….* This won't be the end.

She loves me as much as I love her.

CHAPTER SIXTY FOUR

LUNA

I'm breaking.

Torn apart. I look down to make sure my feet are still on the ground. I'm amazed, but somehow despite the pain, I'm still standing. Agent Dern's voice rings in my head. I don't want to cost Gavin his future. I don't want to be the reason he doesn't get to reach for everything he wants. My hand goes defensively to my stomach.

Pregnant.

My parents are going to kill me. If Gavin is here, it will be one more reason for them to try and strike out at him. If I show up in court in support of Gavin, the judge will take one look at me with my belly swollen with Gavin's child and it might be a nail in Gavin's coffin—despite the fact that I'm eighteen now.

"I can't do this, Gavin."

"What?" he asks, his voice hoarse, and I have to force myself to look up and face him. He starts to blur before me, but I stem the flow of the tears. I can't indulge in them now.

Later.

Later I can cry. Later I can self-destruct and let the misery win.

Not now.

Not when Gavin can see. This is too important.

God, how am I supposed to do this? How can this even be expected of me? I need more time. Time to make my parents understand. Time so they can see how happy Gavin and I can be. Time so they understand he's nothing like they think... Time for Gavin and me to plan our lives around the baby...

I just need time.

"I'm not ready to leave Stone Lake, Gavin. I want to stay here."

His face goes white. He stumbles back like I've hit him, and I guess in some ways I have. My body is trembling, but I can't be sure if it's noticeable from the outside, it's all coming from within.

"We've talked about this. You said you wanted to leave with me, Luna," he pleads and his voice is so quiet, so filled with hurt that it takes my breath.

"I'm not ready. I need… time, Gavin," I tell him.

In my head I keep thinking about everything. I think, if I keep my pregnancy hidden as long as possible, my parents will give up trying to go after Gavin. They need time to get to know him, to see that he's nothing like his father and to see what I do… that Gavin and I were meant to be together.

"If we stay here, you can go to community college and start toward your degree. We can give my parents time to see us together and…"

"And what, Luna? They're not going to magically accept me one day."

"They will see that you're nothing like your father. They'll see how good we are together. It will work out, Gavin. We just need to give it time."

"I can't stay here, Luna. There's nothing for me in Stone Lake. I can't even attend class to finish out my diploma. I'm having to stay in the principal's office and do my work for Christ's sake."

"I'm here, Gavin. Isn't it worth it to try, just for a little while?"

"I want you to go with me, Luna."

"My way is better. We can wait until my parents are more reasonable and—"

"You don't know that they will ever change their mind about me, Luna. Away from here, you and I both get fresh starts. We can do and be whatever we want."

"You can't live your dream if my parents come after us, Gavin and we both know they will if I leave with you."

"We'll deal with it if that happens."

"It's not a matter of if. It's *when* it will happen, Gavin. If we can just hold off for a little while—"

"How long, Luna?"

"Gavin—"

"How much longer do you want me to live in a town that hates me, bumming a couch from my buddy because I don't have a place to live, and hide the fact that I'm in love with you and all while waiting for some miracle to happen and your parents magically accept me."

"Gavin, don't you see—"

"All I see is that you're dreaming. Nothing is going to change by staying in Stone Lake."

"If we leave, my parents will have you arrested!"

"So? I survived once, I'll survive again. They can't keep me locked up. You're eighteen, it will be bogus charges."

"Maybe, but you will still have a record and we did start dating when I was underage."

"Everyone dates young. You're just letting your fear get in your head."

"You're right! I'm scared. I'm terrified. I don't want to be the reason you don't get to be a cop, or a detective, agent, whatever it is. I want you to do what you want. I want you to have your dream."

"You're right, I do want that, but if it doesn't happen, it doesn't happen. I've got other dreams."

"Like what?"

"You, Luna. You're my dream. The only one that matters." His words slice through me like a sharp blade that has been honed and heated for deadly precision.

"Until you grow to hate me," I whisper my voice trembling, hoarse from the tears that want free.

"That won't happen," he says, but he's lying. Maybe I should tell him I'm pregnant. That alone might be enough to make him hate me. I start to… and then stop. I can't even be sure why, but I know I can't tell him.

Not right now.

Not like this.

Maybe it's because I don't want him to hate me, but I think the real reason is I need Gavin to love me.

I want him to love me—like I love him.

I want him to choose me—freely.

I want him to stay, and not just because he's trapped by the girl he knocked up.

And maybe that's not the whole problem. The deal with my parents is there, but time would take care of that, I really believe it would.

"If you stay, we can continue putting money back. We'll be better prepared."

"We're prepared now. I told you that I would take care of you. Are you saying you don't trust me now, Luna?"

"I'm saying I don't want to start our lives together living on the run from my parents and the law."

"Luna," Gavin growls.

"I'm saying I don't want to live in your truck while we get enough money put back to find a place. I'm saying I want time, Gavin, and if you love me, you will give that to me."

"If you love me, you'll go with me."

"*I do love you*. Why are you being like this. It doesn't have to be all or nothing! I'm not saying we won't ever leave. I'm just asking for a little time."

"Luna—"

"I do love you, Gavin. I love you so much. I love you more than you will ever realize. It's just that I'm not willing—"

"And that right there is the difference, Luna. I'm willing to do anything for you."

"Then, stay in Stone Lake with me, Gavin. Just stay here with me for a little while longer. Let me catch my breath. Let me figure things out. Give us a chance."

"I'd give you the stars if I could, Luna. I'd give you anything."

"Gavin—"

"But, I can't give you this. I can't stay here. It will kill me if I'm forced to stay here."

And just like that the world goes dark for me. It feels as if I've died. I can see Gavin standing in front of me, but it's as if everything is just shrouded in a filmy haze of black now.

All hope is gone.

"Then, I guess it's over," I whisper, and I can hear the pain and tears as I say the words.

Can he?

Does he care?

I lose sight of him as the tears finally escape. They fall so hard that they sting, feeling harsh.

"I guess it is," he says, and he looks at me with blue eyes that once held joy and promise and now look as dead as I feel inside.

"Don't go, Gavin," I beg.

"I don't have a choice," he responds and with one last look at me. Then, he turns around and puts one foot in front of the other as every step takes him further away.

I stand there, watching him walk away, barely seeing him through my tears and he doesn't turn around. He doesn't look back.

Not even once.

I stand there and my world ends. The man I love so much that I'm willing to give up everything for him, just so he can reach his goals, is walking away from me and he's not even giving me a backwards glance.

My hand goes to my stomach, the small life that I have inside of me.

I'm all alone now.

I'm pregnant and alone and I know I'll never see Gavin again.

That thought is what finally brings me to my knees, and I fall to the ground, sobs erupting from me, so loud, so filled with anguish that people on the other side of the concession stand come running. I sense them there, I feel someone touching me and hear them asking me questions.

I don't know who it is. I don't know what they ask.

I just know that I feel like I'm slowly dying.

All alone...

CHAPTER SIXTY FIVE

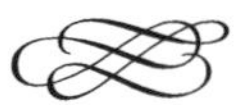

GAVIN

I look at the woman I love, and I see the pain on her face, but all I hear is the fact that she doesn't care enough to put it all on the line for me.

I walk away.

I think I hear her cry out my name, and I try not to look back, but I give in. There's a crowd there now and no sign of her. I feel dead inside. I can't believe this has happened. I can't believe after everything that she can end it like this…

Maybe she never loved me. Maybe I was fooling myself all along.

I walk through the crowd in a daze. I don't see faces, I barely see anything. I just want out of here. There's an old payphone on the side of the school. It's one of the few still around, most everyone uses cellphones these days, but Stone Lake has two of them, one at the school and one outside the grocery store where I work. I've always been glad, because a cellphone isn't something I can afford.

Not now.

Someday I will.

Someday I will be an FBI agent, I'll have money. Women like

Luna will be glad to have me around, will want me and I'll tell them to fuck off.

I'm done with women.

I'm done with caring.

As I make it to the payphone, there are some couples standing around. I see their stares. It doesn't matter that I've been cleared and released by the cops. Most of this town thinks I'm guilty and they don't bother pretending they don't. They leave almost the same time I get there. I guess they don't want to stand close to a murderer. If I didn't feel like I was dying inside, it would be almost comical.

I insert my change and dial the number that Agent Dern gave me. I have it memorized. He was leaving town today, it may be too late.

I hope it's not.

"Agent Dern." His voice is gruff when he answers.

"It's Gavin. Uh... Gavin Lodge."

"What's up, son?"

"Have you left town yet?"

"Heading out in the morning, what's up?"

"I want to go with you."

There's silence on the other line and fear rises inside of me.

He's changed his mind.

"What about the girl?"

"That's not an issue anymore." I grip the phone wishing I could change things, but I can't. She made her choice and now I've made mine.

More silence. He doesn't want me either.

Just like Luna...

I lean against the phone booth. "Forget it, I'll—"

"Where are you?"

"I'm at the high school, getting ready to head to my truck."

"Do you know where my hotel is?"

"Yeah."

"Can you get here okay?"

"Yes, sir."

"Then get here, boy. We'll head out tonight."

"The quicker the better," I tell him, closing my eyes. I hate that the minute they close, Luna's face invades my brain.

I hang up and open my eyes, walking toward my truck. I see Atticus standing in front of me. I walk past him and I don't say one damn word.

He's smiling at me, talking to Larry Richards.

He knows. They both do.

Fuck them.

Fuck them all.

I jump in my truck, rev the engine to life and peel out, leaving Stone Lake and Luna Marshall in my rearview mirror.

EPILOGUE

LUNA

Three Months Later

"You don't look so good."

"You wouldn't look good either if you spent the morning barfing," I mumble.

"You're going to have to tell your parents what is going on, Luna," Atticus says, and he hands me a ginger ale and some saltines.

Every day we meet here at the park lately and he always has ginger ale ready for me. I grab it gratefully. I open it and take a sip, closing my eyes.

"I'll tell Mom soon. Right now I'm okay with wearing big shirts and sweats. Besides it's not like they care. Dad's back to staying gone all the time and Mom is rarely home since she started working again."

After the divorce, Mom got her realtors license and works constantly. Her focus is on moving on with her life now that things have calmed down and the divorce was finalized. I don't know if I will ever feel normal again. First, losing Jules and it feels as if I've lost my parents, too. Then, losing Gavin....

It's all too much to process, so instead I go through the motions of everyday life trying to survive.

"Here, eat the saltines too," he says, taking one of the small single packs and opening it for me. I take a bite, but I don't really want to. Food makes my stomach want to revolt.

It's weird. So much has changed in the last few months. Changes that I never wanted, but I'm finding with life, I've not really been given a choice either. I miss Gavin so much that it has settled into my body like a permanent ache.

Wally gave me a number—a cellphone that Gavin used to call him on. I tried to call it a couple of times. He didn't answer the first time and the second, the phone was disconnected. I got up the nerve to call Agent Dern once. He told me Gavin was doing good and praised me for doing the right thing.

I couldn't very well beg him to tell Gavin to come and get me after that. Instead, I hung up. I miss Jules so much that I don't even know how to express it. There are times in one's life that you truly need your best friend. Right now I need mine so much there are no words. I don't know how to get past the loss I feel. There's a hole in my heart where her and Gavin both resided. *She was my best friend.* Now she's gone, and I will never get her back. No one can replace her. I just don't understand why.

"I'm sorry, Luna."

"It doesn't matter," I tell him and it's true. Nothing really matters anymore. I put the crackers on the bench beside me, unable to stomach more than a bite.

"I'm still sorry. Can I do anything to make it better?"

"Do you hear from Gavin?"

Only Gavin could make things better. I miss him. I ache so deeply to hear his voice. To have him call me Moonbeam. Mom called me that one day and I lost it. I blew up at her and she didn't understand why. I never told her.

How could I explain it to her without giving away my secret?

"You need to forget him, Luna."

"I love him, Attie."

I will always love Gavin.

"Yeah well, he obviously didn't love you. If he did, he never would have left you."

"I pushed him away." I did this to myself–to all of us. Gavin, me and our baby.

"Doesn't matter. If you were my girl, Luna, I'd never leave your side. No matter what, I'd never give up on you."

I'll never be your girl or anyone's for that matter.

But, I don't tell him that.

I'm at the park today, trying to soak up the sunshine, and mostly trying to figure out what I'm going to do. Despite what I told Atticus, I'm not going to be able to keep hiding my pregnancy. I'm going to have to tell my mom. I'm going to have to figure out what I'm going to do about college… life…. And somehow, I'm going to have to give up Gavin. I thought after three months without a word from him, it would have gotten easier.

It hasn't.

It's just been harder. Every day I wake up, I miss him more.

"Luna! Did you hear?" Meghan comes running toward us.

"Hear what?" Atticus asks Meghan as she makes it to us.

That's another strange thing. I thought I hated Meghan because of the way she moved in on Darren, knowing he was dating Jules, but she's really become a good friend and one that I truly need now. She also discovered that Darren was an asshole who was cheating on her and Jules with Marie Ison.

"They arrested Darren this morning."

"Darren?"

"Yeah, they have proof he's the one that killed Jules."

"Proof?" Atticus asks.

"Yeah, I guess they found a witness that saw Darren and Jules fighting near the place where they found her body."

"Holy shit," Atticus says.

Pain shoots down my back. It's so intense that I can't seem to catch my breath.

"You're telling me. I can't believe I dated that monster," Meghan says.

"Just because they were arguing, doesn't mean he did it," I tell him, finally able to talk now that the pain has eased.

"I guess they also found the knife she was stabbed with in his car," Meghan says. "It still weirds me out that I rode in that car," she adds with a shudder.

"I hope they lock him away for life," Atticus growls.

"Me too, I guess," Meghan responds.

"Does that mean you don't think he did it?" I ask, moving around and pressing back against the bench that I'm sitting in because I can feel the pain there again. I've been hurting all day, but not like this.

Maybe I overdid it yesterday when I helped Mom clean house?

"I don't know. The Darren I knew was a dumb ass. It's strange, because we dated for a while and I never got psycho-killer vibes from him at all. Though to be fair, I never got the I'm cheating on you with the biggest ho in the school vibes either," she adds with a flip of her hair.

"Like you would know," Atticus says.

"I'm serious! I get more psycho vibes from you."

"Me?"

"Please, the way you always show up the moment your name is mentioned? It's creepy."

"Whatever."

"I'm just stating the truth, Attie, and I know I've said it a hundred times, but he told me that him and Jules had broken up, or I would have never started talking to him."

I shrug, because it's not like it matters now. Nothing is going to bring Jules back. Hopefully they will make sure Darren won't hurt anyone ever again. I close my eyes as a wave of nausea rolls through me. I close my eyes to fight it and then I gasp out loud as white-hot pain slices through me, centering at the bottom of my stomach. It's so hard that I moan out from the intensity.

"Luna? What's wrong?" Attie asks.

"Luna? Are you okay?"

"I don't... *Oh God,*" I end up crying out as pain even fiercer than before hits me. My body jerks from the force behind it.

"Luna!" I hear Meghan cry.

"Call 911, Meghan," Attie urges, panic laced in his voice.

I hear them, but I can't focus on them. Wave after wave of pain slides through me now and I can't catch my breath.

"What's wrong with her?"

"I don't know. Call 911, Meghan."

"Attie, she's bleeding." I hear her. I shake my head in denial, but I can feel the warmth slide down my legs, and I focus just enough to look down at the white dress that I'm wearing. Deep, bright red color blossoming against the white. I cry out in pain and denial...

And then everything goes black.

THE END

(FOR NOW)

Turn the page for the prologue to Luna & Gavin's conclusion—
When You Were Mine

PROLOGUE

WHEN YOU WERE MINE

Thirteen Years Later
Gavin

"Why did you leave me, Gavin? I needed you."

I jerk awake. My heart beating rapidly, and a cold, clammy sweat covering my body. I throw my legs over the side of the bed, bend down almost to my knees, my hands holding my head. I breathe deep, until I get a hold of myself, then I get up and walk into my bathroom. I turn the shower nozzle until it's definitely more cold than hot and get in.

The icy water runs over my body forcing any urge to sleep out of my system. I grab the body wash and rub it against my face and neck, my eyes closed tightly.

Luna's face is there waiting.

It never fails. You would think after thirteen years she wouldn't haunt me. It doesn't happen all the time, but anytime I have this nightmare, she's there waiting for me in my mind… torturing me.

Sometimes the craziest things can bring on the nightmare. I'll see someone on the street that reminds me of Luna. I'll hear someone laugh and it sounds exactly like her. Other times it's a sunset that reminds me of one I watched with her on that old dock years ago. Tonight's nightmare wasn't because of any of those.

It was because of the orders I got from Quantico.

Another murder.

That's nothing new. It's my job and I've been doing it long enough to know that there is nothing surprising. People are good and bad, but there are some that are evil to their very core. Those are the people I hunt. That's what I do.

My hand goes automatically to the scar on my side.

That's what almost killed me…

No, getting orders from Quantico, is nothing new. Although, it usually revolves around cases in and near Montana, since that's where I work the majority of time. I work out of the Montana field office, so that's to be expected.

Today the orders weren't about Montana. Tonight they want me to go to Maine.

Christ.

I never wanted to step foot back in Maine.

Never.

I get out of the shower, turning it off and reach for a towel. I pat myself dry enough and then hook it around my body, walking out and going to the phone. The bedside clock says three in the morning. It's too fucking late to be calling, but I do.

"This better be good, Kid," Lawrence says when he answers.

"Don't pretend you were sleeping."

"Hell no. I wouldn't care if I was sleeping. You interrupted my drinking."

"Did you know?"

"Know what?" he asks.

"Know that Brass was going to order me to go to Maine."

"Fuck."

"You can say that again," I mutter.

I hear him take another drink and slam a glass or maybe a whole damn bottle down.

"What part?"

"Stone fucking Lake," I answer, the words feeling as if they burn my throat as I say them.

"You could tell them no."

"You know that won't work, Dern."

"Yeah, I know. What are you going to do?"

"Go to Stone Lake. They think it's the Cremator."

"They should have never named that son of a bitch," Lawrence grumbles. "Just gives these sick fucks a taste of fame."

"Yeah, probably. Christ, Lawrence, I don't want to go back to that shithole."

"Wrong. At least don't lie to yourself. You don't want to see *her.*"

"She might not be living in Stone Lake anymore," I tell him and part of me is hoping that's the truth—the other part of me is hoping she's still there. Always where Luna is concerned… there's chaos in my head.

"She is."

"How do you know?" I ask, shocked.

"I might have checked up on her through the years. She's never left Stone Lake."

That's not surprising. She sure wouldn't leave the place for me.

"It doesn't matter anyway. It's been thirteen years. She's probably married with kids," I tell him, even if that thought is painful.

"Probably. Women like that kind of thing."

"What would you know about it?"

"Not a damn thing and that's how I like it. I thought you were following in my footsteps."

"I am."

"Nah. You're just still stuck in the past." He's not entirely right, but he sure as hell ain't wrong either.

"You want to go to Maine with me? They said I could pick my partner."

"You don't need an old has been like me with you, Kid."

"I trust you and that's definitely something I need in Stone Lake."

"There's a reason I'm on a desk. Take Clayton with you. He's a good agent, even if he is a little green."

"I want you."

"Jesus, you're a demanding little prick."

"I'll be at your house tomorrow night, be packed and make sure you're sober."

"Were you always such a bossy S.O.B.?"

"Later, Dern."

"Later, Kid."

I hang up the phone and stare at the wall, seeing nothing just thinking over the turn that my life has taken in the last twenty-four hours.

Whether I want to or not....

I'm coming home to Stone Lake.... And I'm going to see Luna again....

ALSO BY JORDAN MARIE

Stone Lake Series

Letting You Go

When You Were Mine

Savage Brothers MC—Tennessee Chapter

Devil

Diesel

Rory

Savage Brothers MC

Breaking Dragon

Saving Dancer

Loving Nicole

Claiming Crusher

Trusting Bull

Needing Carrie

Devil's Blaze MC

Captured

Craved

Burned

Released

Shafted

Beast

Beauty

Filthy Florida Alphas

Unlawful Seizure

Unjustified Demands

Unwritten Rules

Doing Bad Things

Going Down Hard

In Too Deep

Taking it Slow

Lucas Brothers

The Perfect Stroke

Raging Heart On

Happy Trail

Cocked & Loaded

Knocking Boots

SOCIAL MEDIA LINKS

Keep up with Jordan and be the first to know about any new releases by following her on any of the links below.

Newsletter Subscription
Facebook Reading Group
Facebook Page
Twitter
Webpage
Bookbub
Instagram
Youtube

Text Alerts (US Subscribers Only—Standard Text Messaging Rates May Apply):

Text ***JORDAN*** to 797979 to be the first to know when Jordan has a sale or released a new book.

Made in the USA
Middletown, DE
09 July 2019